My Father's Books

My Father's Books

Luan Starova

Translated by

Christina E. Kramer

THE UNIVERSITY OF WISCONSIN PRESS

Publication of this English translation was made possible, in part,
with support from the
Canadian Macedonian Place Foundation,
Toronto, Canada.

The University of Wisconsin Press
1930 Monroe Street, 3rd Floor
Madison, Wisconsin 53711-2059
uwpress.wisc.edu

3 Henrietta Street
London WCE 8LU, England
eurospanbookstore.com

Originally published in Macedonia as *Tatkovite knigi*, copyright © 1992

Published in France as *Les livres de mon père*, copyright © 1998 Librairie Arthème Fayard

English translation copyright © 2012 The Board of Regents
of the University of Wisconsin System

Printed in the United States of America

Library of Congress Cataloging-in-Publication Data
Starova, Luan.
[Tatkovite knigi. English]
My father's books / Luan Starova; translated by Christina E. Kramer.
p.   cm.
"Originally published in Macedonia as Tatkovite knigi, copyright 1992"—T.p. verso.
ISBN 978-0-299-28794-8 (pbk.: alk. paper)
ISBN 978-0-299-28793-1 (e-book)
1. Starova, Luan—Childhood and youth.
2. Authors, Macedonian—20th century—Biography.
I. Kramer, Christina Elizabeth.   II. Title.
PG1196.29.T37A313   2012
891.8′193—dc23
[B]

2011046137

Contents

The Books and My Father's Friends

Father's Books, Migrations, Stalinism, the Balkan Wall

Part Two

The Margins of My Father's Books:
The Constantinople Dream, in Search of Lost Time

Time Discovered

Perhaps the Real Ending

Translator's Note

Fortunate are the nations that have no history (he recalled the words of a certain French historian), yet, as he himself concluded, there is no nation without history.

Luan Starova recalls his father's words as he sets out to explore the history of his family across the Balkans and through the turbulent years of the twentieth century. In his multivolume Balkan saga he treats themes of history, displacement, and identity. *My Father's Books* is the first in this series. Following the thread of his parents' lives through the fifty-year period from 1926 to 1976, Starova presents a series of eighty overlapping fragments of memory. As he attempts to untangle the family's intersecting religious, linguistic, national, and cultural histories, he seeks to untangle the history of the Balkans as new nations arose in the wake of the collapse of the Ottoman Empire.

In these vignettes, or fragments of memory, told from the point of view of the child of parents who moved across the Balkans, across territories that are now Turkey, Greece, Albania, and Macedonia, Starova attempts to answer questions of cultural inheritance, linguistic identification, and a sense of national or, better, supranational belonging.

One of the recurring themes in this book is that of labyrinths, crossroads, and the flow of history. He sees his parents and those around them try to make sense of and to survive in the complex political history of the twentieth-century Balkans, from the end of Ottoman rule through the Stalinist years of shock workers and collectivization, always amid continually shifting ideologies and borders. Another of the enduring themes is Starova's father's love of books—how the life of the mind is the common language that unites people. His father's library is his true fatherland, the country of the mind, borderless, boundless, and bondless.

Starova also focuses on the theme of the Janissary past. The elite Janissary corps, the Ottoman standing army, was built up through a system of conscription in which non-Muslim children were abducted, forced to convert to Islam, then raised to become soldiers. Starova explores the implications for individuals who are forced to sacrifice family, language, and culture to gain prestige through working as a tool of the empire. What must be sacrificed for personal salvation and advancement?

Luan Starova was born in 1941 in the town of Pogradec, located on the Albanian shores of Lake Ohrid. Two years later the family left Albania forever, moving first to Struga, on the shores of Lake Ohrid, and then later to Macedonia's capital city, Skopje, then part of Yugoslavia. After completing his BA in literature from the University of Saints Kiril and Metodij in Skopje, he went on to receive his MA and PhD in French and comparative literature from the University of Zagreb. He has worked as a university professor and later served as Macedonia's ambassador to France. He is a member of the Macedonian Academy of Sciences. His Balkan saga has been widely acclaimed and has won numerous awards both in Macedonia and internationally. Surprisingly, although Starova's works have been translated into more than a dozen languages, this is the first of his works to appear in English.

Because of his unique position as an Albanian writing in Macedonian and Albanian, Starova's work belongs to the growing literary canon in both languages. His voice provides a unique perspective. Too often we read of disunity and violence in the Balkans. Starova allows us a window into the human interactions, shared humanity, and common fate of people buffeted by a century of war. He never loses his gentle yet powerful voice, which speaks to the dignity of his parents, his family, the people of the Balkans. Through these fragments of memory he creates a vivid whole, showing the maze of interacting, intertwined fates of the Balkan peoples in a new light, one that connects this region to the intellectual and literary currents of Europe.

I am grateful to the following for their editorial assistance and advice: Paul Franz, Madeline Levine, David Kramer, Victor Friedman, and Martin Sokolovski. For financial assistance in support of the publication of this manuscript I thank Canadian Macedonian Place Foundation, Toronto, Canada.

CHRISTINA E. KRAMER

Toronto, 1 May 2011

My Father's Books

The end of the book is, perhaps, the end of time.
Edmond Jabès

*F*rom my father and mother's half century of life together, I inherited—
for my entire life—a great treasure of quiet, created in the silences
between the raps of fate at the family's doors. In the life that my parents
passed on to me it remained for me to search out the source of this quiet
and, with the few words that sprang forth, to create the history of my
family, which, at the same time, represented the fifty-year period of
Balkan history from 1926 to 1976.

After my father's death I did not go near his books for years. Old
manuscripts, yellowed books, carried from every corner of the earth,
lived on according to the order my father had given them. Arranged
along the shelves of his library, they radiated their final significance . . .

In the course of time, as my first memories faded, I began to move
my father's books around. I would take a book and place it in a different
spot. Unconsciously, I upset the order of the books in Father's library,
so much that I could no longer bring it back . . .

But, one day, my father called out from one of the books I had
moved! My memories became confused. I could see him tracing along
the old order of the books. After he discovered the true place of each
displaced book, he began to read . . .

My father was a passionate reader but an even more passionate smoker; he would get so engrossed in reading every page that he would forget about the ash of his cigarette.

And today, when I leaf through the pages of his books, in the manuscripts where ash intermingles most with the letters on the page, his voice lives on . . .

LUAN STAROVA

February 1986

Part One

My Father, Our Family, the Books

Love

Each new book awakened great joy in my father's soul. We lived in a small house, and we were a large family. Every inch of space was filled with objects and with our presence. There was no space where even a book could be set down without our accustomed order being disturbed.

My mother had cause to be angry at each new book's arrival, mainly because of our tight quarters but also because of our diminishing family resources. However, like a true magician of our family's hearth, my mother always discovered some new space for each new book somewhere other than in my father's overflowing bookcases. She also became the unseen librarian of my father's books. Whenever my father searched for a book he was not quite sure he owned, my mother would slip away unnoticed to the built-in cabinet to retrieve the one he was looking for and then discreetly place it on my father's desk while he, still grasping at a thought he wished to formulate, continued looking distractedly along the shelves of his library in search of the book. He would be pulled from this state by my mother's calm steps, which broke the silence and then receded like a whisper, informing my father that the book had been found . . .

The Fate of the Books

Habent sua fata libelli.

Of all the tangible things that remained in the world at the end of my father's life, a possible proof of the lost past is his books. It is also possible that one of the secrets of my parents' durable, harmonious marriage was my mother's good-natured encouragement and support of my father's love for his books and her transformation into a kind of holy guardian of his library. It is, in fact, from the pages of my father's movable library that the history of my family, constructed by my parents, can most clearly be read and understood. Wherever we were driven by the path of migrations and the instinct for family survival, my father's books accompanied us.

A new book was like a newborn in the family, with its own place in our family's life, or like a new footpath that allowed us to walk yet farther along life's long road.

During the family's frequent migrations, during the frequent changes of Balkan borders, which often fatally and tragically split the destinies of individuals, families, and nations, we left everything behind except the books.

The books also befriended us in those moments when there was only enough time for life itself to be saved, as if hidden on one of their pages was the prophecy of the family's salvation.

Differences

Even before I had learned to read and write, my father's books, guarded by my mother's wakeful eye, served as my playthings. Since then I have had a passion for the large, tightly bound, multicolored volumes and have reveled in them with no thought as to whether I would ever read them.

While still an untaught child I could easily "read" various scripts. Even at that time, I "read" that my father had books written in Arabic, Cyrillic, and Latin letters. At that time, all books were the same at first glance, but when I opened them they immediately became different from one another. But these "differences," texts in different alphabets, began to have significance for me, to have specificity, before I had yet entered the world of interpretable signs.

The various alphabets appeared to me as the first mirrors of fate in which, in various ways, I would be reflected and would discover myself. I had to discover in the three different shapes of symbols in the manuscripts that one unique form with which I would identify, the one fated to remain until the end of my life forever in the center of the labyrinth.

The Garden

*A*s I matured, something changed in my relationship to my father's books, to the yellowed registers with their handwriting that nearly over-flowed, ready to spill off the page, to the peculiar deeds of lost property, decrees, diplomas with pressed wax seals, miscellaneous certificates, testaments, books of all sorts.

We lived in the house of an old bey, just beyond the path leading off the old wooden bridge that connected the theater, with its classical architecture, to a covered market. The old house still retained the con-tours of both Oriental and European architecture, here wonderfully combined in a kind of synthesis that could be preserved in this way only in the Balkans. But whatever style it was, this house by the river was filled with the vibrancy of the landscape and the indeterminacy of the water's current, the flow of passing time.

My mother always took tremendous pains to maintain order in our house, where the tendency was for things to spread out all over the place. She would sweep the house tenaciously, starting from the long courtyard wall, then moving on to the large rooms, stopping finally at the overhanging enclosed balcony. After a short rest, she would then set out to bring order to the fenced-in garden, where it seemed as if space itself had been captured, beauty contained, and the natural flow of light confined. As if to compensate for all that had been lost due to its en-closure, the small garden had a complicated mosaic of winding stone pathways, and in the center a small fountain that continuously sprayed the roses, the carnations, and the basil, to which my mother remained most loyal. In this garden my mother sowed her own restlessness along with the seeds of flowers.

After the family's great wanderings, it was there, within these garden walls, that a space of momentary calm was captured before the challenge of fate's new demands.

The Fountain

A beautiful book is always about a successful family.

folk saying

*W*hat comes most often to the surface of my memory, other than the garden with its fountain constantly murmuring some piece of our family's history, is the overhanging balcony, which seemed to keep the house on the edge of departure, of flight.

After sleepless nights, my father would emerge onto the balcony, often with his gaze fixed on the rapid waters of the river. Here, before sunrise, his thoughts would coalesce into the glimmer of a new idea that had long been gestating in his consciousness.

The path of my father's significant thoughts ended on this balcony. It was here also that sleep would overcome him, letting the house slip into a kind of silence. My mother would cover him with a thin blanket to protect his light sleep. Sometimes, late at night, he would wake out of a silence broken by the restless slumbering of the children long since asleep in the nearby rooms. As if catching a trace of the energy liberated by our sleeping, he would fall into a new, deep, fresh, and fervent reading. Thus, our falling into sleep was, more often than not, his awakening.

My mother faithfully followed the comings and goings in the life of the family, and inside she fervently sensed that my father was on the verge of some new decision of significance for all of us.

The Balcony

When she saw a book that Father had left behind on the balcony, my mother knew that the day before, in that moment between dream and reality, in a flash of insight, her husband must surely have come to that long-sought-after decision, the decision that now in the daylight he must undertake. Then, tenderly, as if prolonging my father's touch, Mother would take the book that had been left behind and place it carefully on one of the shelves in the cabinet built into the balcony walls rather than in the library, where nearly all of Father's books were arranged.

In the center of the large, windowless wall of the living room, the room that actually adjoined the balcony, there was a two-winged wooden cabinet, which evoked for us children the unfailing illusion of a world beyond, on the other side of the wall, in the balcony cabinet . . .

That cabinet was rarely opened, and therefore it, more than anything else, sparked our childhood curiosity. It was always locked up tight, with its own lock and a separate padlock.

The cabinet was a sort of annex to my father's library, its heart, for there inside it were the oldest manuscripts, handwritten sacred books, rare geographic maps of imagined Balkan states, the family's precious documents: papers that proved the family's identity.

The cabinet was wide, deep, boundless. Most often, it was my father who went in there, more rarely, my mother, and then only when she needed to free the books of their collected dust. When my father entered the cabinet, we children had the feeling that he was entering some new dimension of time in the labyrinth of his manuscripts.

We children thought that there, in my father's cabinet, in that labyrinth of lost time—how quickly time was lost in the Balkans—were to be found the hurt books, those damaged by too much reading, too much time.

As soon as he had "cured" a particular one of his hurt books, my father would return it to its usual place in the library.

My father ordinarily kept the cabinet locked up, and he left the key with my mother in case the books should rise up . . .

The Cabinet

One morning, when my mother had gone to the market and my brothers had gone off in various directions, either to school or out with friends, I remained at home alone, absolutely alone. Naturally, my eyes drifted to the cabinet. I noticed that, for the first time, the key was still in the lock. I was overcome with excitement. I turned the key. Our family Babel was opened; it was as if I had entered into the realm of some forbidden dream.

The books seemed to be living things, so strongly was I affected by this encounter with them. First, the large encyclopedias caught my eye, and then the old sacred books, the deeds, the scrolls, the family documents. But what most captured my attention were the pages that had multicolored stamps embellished with the shapes of green postmarks.

Who would have known then that in those papers was inscribed the whole of my family's odyssey?

It was as if there, on torn and intact stamps, resided all the resurrected monarchs, despots, and emperors of fallen empires who at various times had ruled my family's fate. They were now enclosed, vanquished, abandoned in Father's big cabinet. I was prepared at once to deal with their thwarted power, to detach them from my father's, from the family's, papers. This was, in my eyes, to be their ultimate downfall.

I tore the stamps from these vital family documents, and, in so doing, I defaced the identity of our family, which had been sustained and safeguarded with so much difficulty through so many Balkan storms.

I imposed my own order on my father's documents and manuscripts. In those yellowed pages the traces of Balkan time were most deeply engraved.

In the Balkans everyone wanted to steal our time. In those days I was under the illusion that our lost, unlived time was imprisoned in the cabinet with the rare books.

Engrossed in my task, I cut out small pictures from what were perhaps the only encyclopedias in this region of the Balkans. I unglued tax stamps from the birth certificates, as if liberating them from their ties to past regimes.

Later I traded the small stamps that had marked the family's most significant documents for stamps belonging to the neighborhood children. In exchange for stamps with pictures of fallen kings and old coins with faces of Roman emperors, also fallen, I took stamps of current rulers. In the Balkans such trade was always bountiful.

Sometimes I exchanged two kingdoms for one, sometimes even three. That's how quickly their value fell.

I left the cabinet in unparalleled disarray, having destroyed, as if forever, my father's ordering of time. I had been inside the cabinet for a long time. As I emerged, I met my mother's frantic gaze. Rarely had I seen my mother crying. All the doors and windows of the old house were open. The crosscurrents had carried my father's papers out of the cabinet, and they flew everywhere, though mostly piling up on the balcony. Mother chased them in a frenzy, not letting a single one fly out of the house. After she had gathered them up and closed all the windows, she entered the cabinet. And what did she see there! She remained in that cabinet an entire eternity.

She restored order as best she could, but there was no way she could return the former order to the papers and old books. There had been no greater upheaval in the history of our family than those moments when what had been held most sacred was nearly lost. During the era in which my family lived in the Balkans there had been two world wars, civil wars, great earthquakes and epidemics, forced migrations—all hard raps of fate on the doors of our family. We had even watched, helpless, as those closest to us had died and departed.

Neither before, nor in the years that followed, did I ever see my mother so frantic, so dismayed.

These dramatic events brought white into my mother's hair. Yes, her white hairs were a veritable archive of our family life.

Her stifled cries of anguish and insurmountable pain pressed to the very roots of her hair. In her life she had suffered many blows, many life-and-death battles; her body had endured frequent pregnancies; she had painfully paid the price for maintaining the family. In her life she had suffered and endured a great deal.

Her whole life was spent fighting to keep her children alive. We children had become accustomed to seeing death enter the family and depart again and to watching Mother wear herself out in battle with it. For her this episode of the books was yet another torment.

Identity

*M*y mother had her own ritual way of greeting my father when he came home from work. She would never press him at once about the daily household worries. She always waited for just the right moment. Every minute was filled with the essence of their entire shared life, and there was no need for them to surrender peaceful moments. It did not make sense to spoil the present moment with what had to come, what had to happen anyway. This was almost sacred in my parents' life. No two moments could coexist within any single moment of their lives. When fear settled on the family because of something that had to occur, a sort of mysterious fatalism that accompanies every family that is compelled to move, my mother knew how to make a kind of internal compromise with the times, the good and the bad. She had a built-in mechanism that allowed her to endure both fortune and misfortune. This was true even after my massacre of the papers and books in the cabinet.

When my father returned home that day, he calmly ate his dinner, surrounded by the rhythm and habitual quiet that radiated through our family whenever he came from work. Then he took his customary late afternoon nap. As time passed, the delayed consequences of the events in the cabinet weighed on me ever more heavily.

In the silent, early evening hours that first entered the house through the balcony, my father turned toward the cabinet to fetch some book, and thus complete his usual daily schedule on this day as well. He pulled the cabinet doors wide open.

I remained riveted to the spot where I stood: it was impossible to move, to run away, to save myself. My father was at first unable to detect the massacre I had carried out because my mother had done what she could to salvage much of the former organization. He found the book he was looking for and now began to look for a certain document. Even had he noticed that something had occurred in the cabinet, he would not have wanted to believe such a thing were possible. By some miracle, he immediately found the document he wanted. But when he noticed that the stamps had been unglued and torn from the document, what had happened slowly dawned on him.

His face went blank. My mother watched him in silence. It was like this only when someone in the family died. This, however, was akin to the death of the entire family. How to prove our identity, which was constantly verified, using documents with stamps removed? Had the documents been yellowed, torn, or crumpled, he could have dealt somehow with those who check identity papers, but with their stamps torn off, with their figureheads removed, it became difficult, uncertain. Adding to our misfortune, the stamps had also been detached from the documents establishing our newly acquired citizenship. Who could make sense of this?

I was small then, and I felt even smaller inside. For the first time, I waited in the corner to be punished for my misconduct. My father and mother had never raised a hand against us children. They had calmed us with their quiet. That is how it often was when life was difficult: the storm was calmed from within, in my parents' souls.

My father did not raise his hand, but I will never forget the expression of indescribable pain on his face, something I think I have inherited for eternity.

This tragic event of my childhood, the massacre of my father's old "hurt" books, has somehow marked the entire course of my life, as if I were sentenced then to expiate this great sin forever.

In the course of time, my great misadventure with the books, which I experienced at the very dawn of my life, resolved into a great friendship between my father and me, into love, and into a shared devotion to books.

It was perhaps vital for the maintenance of our friendship that I would solve with books the conflict that had arisen between us because of his books.

When I began to write and to publish, my father became my most regular, most valued, and most critical reader. And when I lost my father in my adult years, I was certain that I had lost my most faithful reader, the living connection with books, the central impetus for my writing. But as I made peace with this irretrievable loss, I continued to seek him in his books and in the books I continued to write . . .

The Life of the Books

*A*s years passed and my father began to buy more books than he could read, I detected a trace of pleasure in my mother's expression, not only because there might be more space in the house but also because my father might perhaps have some rest from books in his remaining years. Still, when my father really began to divest himself of his books, my mother's joy was short-lived. She had not expected that at all, at least not to such an extent.

The truth is that, for my mother, a house without books would have meant peace, cleanliness, less dust, more air, but, on the other hand, it would have meant the beginning of a silence that would replace the bustle of life and would have suggested some kind of end . . .

For the first time in his life, my father recognized his powerlessness, though not defeat, in the realm of books. He had long believed that he would live longer than the books. But he now perceived his weakness: it was impossible to read them all before the end of his life. He finally settled on a small practical library, hoping he would read at least these before the end . . .

The Death
of the Manuscript

As old age galloped across his wrinkled forehead and his eyes lost their former vibrancy, my father journeyed with ever-increasing difficulty through his Ottoman manuscripts. He took to using all kinds of reading lenses. He engaged in an increasingly enfeebled battle with the symbols that hid from his determined gaze and that he hunted down with the power of his intellect.

And so it was every day. When at daybreak there would appear at the doorway of our house a translator of old Ottoman manuscripts, one who believed that Father must hold the key to their interpretation, Mother would whisper sadly, looking at my father's exhausted body moving now mostly by force of spirit, that here came yet another tormenter of her life's companion.

But when the translators spread out the documents on the table and they had begun a conversation about the old manuscript, my father would truly come to life; his blood flowed more strongly, opening a pathway through his withered veins. This could best be seen in his long, desiccated hands, in his broad forehead, his long neck. His eyes traveled brightly across the manuscript. From somewhere he found strength; he would swallow his saliva periodically, and then, with dignity, as if pulling something from within him and from past time, he would solve the elusive riddle that for centuries had kept the manuscript lifeless . . .

The younger translators would note down with satisfaction every word that came from my father's mouth, and my mother would enter the room more frequently, fearing that some burst of pleasure from the translators would extinguish my father's life.

A Secret

On the topmost shelf of my father's library were several volumes with beautiful leather covers, clearly different from the other, more ordinary books. We children secretly took advantage of our access to the books.

When my father was at work we would take down a book that we did not know how to read, or one rich with pictures, and later return it to its place. We never made a mistake. My father knew that his books disappeared and then returned to their places, and, inwardly pleased, he never stopped our game.

Soon, nearly all the books had been examined; only those on the uppermost shelf remained untouched. One morning, when we were certain that we were alone in the house, we went into Father's library. We stacked one chair on top of another. Supported by my brothers, I reached up to the highest shelf. As I touched the books on the top shelf, I felt myself losing my balance, and, with books in hand, I tumbled down. At that moment Mother, who had returned early from the market, was entering the house, and my startled brothers let go of the chairs.

I found myself on the floor with the half-opened books; from their pages escaped a heretofore-unknown aroma, as if a bygone era pressed within their pages had suddenly been set free. On some of them shone small blue and golden stars that connected the faded black and brown markings spread across the pages, revealing that the books had been written by hand. It seemed as if these marks also encircled the tiny blue stars and the other miniature designs.

Alarmed, my mother entered the library. She too had known that we secretly availed ourselves of our father's books, but she never imagined that we would reach up to that top shelf.

We children had no idea what sort of books these were, and therefore we could not understand my mother's odd behavior. She paid no attention to my fall but picked up the fallen books; for the first time in our lives we saw her silently shedding tears.

What had happened?

What had fallen out of the books?

What sort of impenetrable meaning radiated from these books with their unusual markings and sky-blue drawings, with their countless little shining stars, that had seemingly tumbled down from heaven?

Mother, gazing at us as we stood confused and in tears, gathered up the fallen books and wiped away the dust, then together we returned them to their place. In my father's library there remained many secrets that could not be fully revealed.

Learning
about the Deities

Since I was not grounded in any religion, I was ruled by a vague atheism that generally left me indifferent to any religious affiliation.

My parents held a discreet and calm faith to which they never called attention in their actions; rather, a need to believe in a singular all-powerful force had coalesced in them after so many deaths in the family, so many relocations to who knows where, so many new adjustments.

Thus, I remained without a basic religious education, nor did I possess my parents' calm faith, especially during difficult times in my life. It was perhaps because of this that I was often extreme in my thoughts about religion: either I vehemently rejected the existence of God, or, in times of misfortune, particularly when I lost those closest to me, without whom my life lost its prior meaning, I was prepared to curse the fate that had left me a religious outcast.

Later, in my frequent travels throughout the world, I entered cathedrals, pagodas, synagogues, and mosques, all with the same feelings of restrained piety; then, when I attempted to introduce the peacefulness of this holy quiet into my writing, I noted with increasing frequency my estrangement from religion. I sometimes wrote absurd and poignant sketches. In one of my stories I called upon the gods to save the life of an unfortunate character. After reading "The Death of the Deities," my father, a devoted citizen of my manuscripts, gently rebuked me, his voice a quiet human bell, still reverberating within me: "Since you don't know they exist, my son, why have you pronounced the gods dead?"

My Father's Fatherlands

*I*n those rare moments when, bent over his opened books, he considered his fate, seeking solutions to the Balkan history of his family, in those moments when he thought he was fully prepared to begin writing the history of the Balkans through the decline of the three empires (Ottoman, Fascist, and Stalinist) with which the life of his family had collided, my father began to ask himself which was his fatherland: the fatherland of his ancestors or the fatherland of his descendants?

He was deeply convinced, and no one and nothing could dissuade him from this belief, that his library remained his ultimate fatherland. It was filled with books in various languages, in various scripts, from various eras. Here, too, was the great globe he rotated when he was unable to confirm his true homeland.

Mother was not concerned about the family's survival so long as she could see my father in the library, at peace in his own country. If she sensed that the pages of a book were being disturbed, if Father's shadow played across the walls of the room, then my mother feared another exodus was ahead . . .

Before departures to yet-unknown destinations, my father would often mark down the tally of his lost, discovered, abandoned, forgotten, and renewed fatherlands, states, and monarchies. One could see how many there had been in his life by looking in his documents at the heads of different leaders on the canceled administrative stamps.

Although the Ottoman Empire changed my father's original faith, and at that time religion was the equal of state and fatherland, it did not become his country. Atatürk's Turkey was expected to become my father's home after his studies in Constantinople and his brief meeting with Atatürk himself; my father's mother's Turkish identity may also have had an influence. When she sent him off to Constantinople, to her people, she could have realized her distant dream, aware that she herself would never catch up to them in their great escape. But Father returned to the Balkans.

His fatherland became Albania, an independent state with an uncertain future enmeshed in Balkan misfortunes. But it was not to remain his fatherland for long.

When his frail native country became entrapped in the web of Fascism, Father consciously gave up his fatherland and crossed the closest border. Between Fascism and the Communism that loomed, he chose the loss of his homeland. Ultimately, he could not avoid Communism in either his native country or his adopted one. But here, in Yugoslavia, liberation from Stalinism came much sooner than for our relatives across the border in Albania, who suffered beneath it much longer, much, much longer. While my father was indeed saved from Stalinism, he remained an émigré of his old country. As emigrants, we were, in fact, at some sort of Balkan way station, a place to sojourn before continuing along pathways of resettlement across the ocean.

My father accepted his new citizenship and freed himself from further phantom emigrations. We did not become citizens of America or Australia or even of New Zealand, as others did who crossed the border after us. After assuming citizenship, my father did not believe, even in his dreams, that as a new citizen of the People's Republic of Macedonia, then part of the Federal People's Republic of Yugoslavia, with his old Ottoman law degree, he would become a Socialist judge in a single step. As a new immigrant, not to mention a non-party member, one who did not wish to be counted in the government structures as a minority representative chosen by quota, Father knew that he would not be able to advance far in a legal career and move up in the judicial hierarchy. Fortunately, while working in the Institute of National History, he discovered Ottoman-era documents from Bitola, Turkish court administrative records dating from the sixteenth to the nineteenth centuries, and thus secured his future and the future of his children.

My father ended his life as a citizen of the Socialist Federal Republic of Yugoslavia and of the Socialist Republic of Macedonia. He did not live to see the breakup of Yugoslavia, which gave his offspring citizenship in a new country, the Republic of Macedonia. First they were a minority, then an ethnic minority, and now a nationality, without ever sufficiently understanding the significance of each new designation.

And so, in my father's family, in the space of a single generation, fatherlands changed more than once, citizenship changed even more frequently, together with an equal number of designations for civic status. Too much for one generation! But not so in the Balkans, where this and even more were possible. What lies in store for the future generations of the family God alone knows, as my mother would have said while she was still alive, holding her final citizenship.

My Father's Languages

*W*hen it came time at school for me to choose a foreign language, I asked my father, then deeply engrossed in a book, whether I should study French, English, Russian, or German, just one, or two simultaneously, and, if so, which ones? My father set his glasses down right at the passage where he had stopped in his reading, his tender glance caressed the depths of my soul, and he quietly said, "My dear son, there's no big secret. Study any language at all, but study one rather than several, just learn it as it needs to be learned. Enter into the depths of any language, and eventually you will learn that at heart, all languages touch one another, they stem from the same human root . . ."

That's what my father said to me, and that was enough for me to settle on French alone, setting other languages aside.

After saying this, my father once again immersed himself in his old texts, the judicial records from Bitola, written in the old official language of the sixteenth century. I thought then about what languages were my father's, how he had acquired that knowledge that, in the end, he bequeathed to me, like something found after long searching through linguistic labyrinths.

In what language does one write, cry, dream, suffer?

There were still countless such questions I could have asked my father, but their answers were impressed upon me through the slow revelation of his books' secrets.

My father had a strange, uncertain, complex, and elusive linguistic history, one that was not exceptional in the Balkans for individuals or groups of people.

My father's native language was Turkish. His mother instilled it in him with all its mellowness and sonority. It was a different Turkish from that used in everyday official communication by the Turkish governmental leaders in our Albanian lakeside town. The local people were opposed to my father's type of Turkish, and they kept their distance. The reasons for this could be sensed with ease but understood only with difficulty. My father's mother, with her natural gentleness and unobtrusiveness, lessened this distance.

Although the Ottoman Empire was setting and one could sense its demise, while the Albanian language was on the rise, seeking its definitive form, my father, studying in Constantinople, became engrossed and absorbed in his Turkish mother tongue, while remaining at the same time, due to a different family tradition, faithful to the Albanian language. And so in Constantinople, as he followed his mother's dream, he became imbued with both Ottoman and modern Turkish, but he could not free his destiny from the paradoxes that followed him at every turn of his life.

Just when my father had mastered Ottoman Turkish and the old Arabic script and had perfected his calligraphy, Atatürk abolished the old script and introduced a Latin orthography, to which my father now had to become accustomed. Up till then he had written from right to left; now he had to write from left to right. He had beautiful calligraphy in Arabic script; it was not quite so beautiful in Latin letters, and, finally, this same handwriting ended up indecipherable in the Cyrillic alphabet. In his old age, he often jumbled these last two alphabets. When he had occasion to translate an old Turkish document into Macedonian, my father would first rewrite the document in old Arabic script with great pleasure and unparalleled speed. He was like a different person when the document, translated into Macedonian, had to be written in the Cyrillic script. In the end, of course, we children were there for him, and we wrote down Father's completed Macedonian translation.

The final paradox occurred toward the end of his life when his knowledge of Ottoman Turkish, a language for which he had had no use for so long, led him to the greatest discovery of his life—the old Bitola court records, a discovery that my father considered a gift from God because he had remained faithful, as he needed to be, to one language alone.

My Father's Dictionaries

*I*n the final years of his life, as he slowly lost the strength to read, my father became less and less alive. When I saw that he no longer read or commented on the books I brought him, but only held them absently in his hands, appearing to read, taking in some meaning that he alone understood, tears would come unbidden to my eyes. I would gently try to take the book from him and read aloud from the opened page, but this created a different problem, since he could not completely follow what I was reading. Thus I slowly lost my father and he his books.

In a life extended across many languages, my father never attained complete mastery of one language. He had within him the energy of the many languages he knew, that he had studied in depth, compared, and enriched.

Toward the end of his life, as his strength for reading decreased, my father, to our great amazement, continued to learn new languages, to peruse old and new grammars, to buy new dictionaries, to fall into a strange associative language dream. He learned new words, created interlinguistic coinages, believing that he would come at last to his own linguistic eureka, which would enable him to move, when necessary, from one language to another and so be understood by everyone. He died with a dictionary in his hands.

My father died untranslated . . .

The Radio

We had an old radio in the house, one that my father had dragged, as something of greatest value, to the Balkans after his stay in Constantinople.

The radio accompanied us through all our moves. It was shaped like a peacock with its feathers open and fanned wide, as if each feather designated a different radio station. In the center of the radio, actually a bit below the center, in the area of the peacock's head and beak, there was inset a small lighted window with names of cities marked on it.

In the middle of the night my father seemed to visit the designated cities and receive strange messages, which he tried to interpret during the daylight hours and understand in the context of his Balkan destiny.

He listened most often to the BBC. He remembered the messages de Gaulle transmitted to occupied France.

In the wee hours of the morning he searched the radio for that enthralling Arabian spirituality that seemed to carry him off on a magic carpet of memory away from the Balkans to a time of his early youth.

In the morning, my mother, knowing that my father had been listening to the radio all night out on the balcony, always asked the same question: Will there be war? Will there be war? My mother would glance over at us children, who had just woken up.

We children, with our sharp ears, in contrast to my father, who was slowly losing his hearing, clearly heard the radio when he thought he was the only one listening. We could not understand why our father lowered the volume at some stations and raised it at others, always glancing out from the balcony to the street below.

On holidays, especially on the First of May, the Day of the Republic, and the Day of the Army, he would raise the volume, especially during broadcasts of popular and revolutionary songs, as if he wanted to prove the correctness of his political views to the neighbors. This created in him a certain balance, because during the night he listened surreptitiously to those Western stations, reported by the local radio stations to be the broadcasts of spies, imperialists, and capitalists.

When history began to flow quickly through the Balkans, my father became completely transfixed by the radio, somehow wanting to influence the battle taking place over its waves.

The radio transmitted the history of the times in which we lived as much as it absorbed the history of our family.

In the course of time, the old radio lost its former significance for the family, but even after my father's death, my mother continued to clean its little window, as though deep, deep inside it she touched my father's face.

Old Age

When the shell of my father's life began to close and there was only space inside for his solitude, those nearest to him, who he secretly felt had less and less need of him, tried to turn him away from his pact with death.

Nearly all his life, in the evening hours, after the stormy and uncertain day, out on the balcony he loved to sip a glass of rakija and nibble the appetizers that my mother prepared for him, mostly from the vegetables she grew in the small garden behind the house.

This is how he paced his day, his life, and kept his blood circulating. As was his custom, he would smoke a cigarette or two with the Turkish coffee my mother made for him. His closest family members begged and pleaded with him not to drink and smoke so that he would live as long as possible . . .

Once, apparently fed up with these frequent rebukes, he asked one of his doctor sons, "My dear son, you give me wonderful advice not to smoke or drink rakija so I can live longer. So tell me the truth—how many more years of life will you give me if I don't smoke or drink?"

His doctor son, filled with compassion, said to him, "Dad, you are now seventy years old! If you don't drink or smoke, you will reach eighty, but if you continue, you will live four years less."

"In other words, seventy-six," my father calculated. Everyone looked at him with pity, but he stated with self-assurance, "I will keep my pleasures, and until that time, you keep your peace." We all looked at him sadly.

My father lived to be exactly seventy-six years old.

The Books and
My Father's Friends

Eastern Dream and Western Dream

*F*or years, an old man, whom I shall call Mr. K., came to see my father; they were friends.

Their mutual love of old books and manuscripts united them. Both were captive to a great but unrealizable dream. For my father it was an Eastern dream; for Mr. K., a Western one. In a sense they complemented each other. This was cause for agreement and disagreement between them.

My father's dream began when he was a young man in Constantinople. The volcanic explosiveness of his youth coincided with great historical events: the collapse of the Ottoman Empire, when the division of the Balkans, anticipated for half a millennium, finally occurred. Here it was that paths opened up for him leading to all of life's many opportunities. On one occasion he even found himself at a meeting with Kemal Atatürk. My father would feel the reverberations of these moments to the end of his life.

Throughout his life my father would turn over in his mind the words that Atatürk had spoken: "You young intellectuals in Constantinople, we will need you to set us on the new path in our history, the path toward Europe." It was as if in Constantinople my father had found himself set before a labyrinth of intersecting paths.

When my father returned to the Balkans, he found an exit from the family's old labyrinth and an entryway into the labyrinth of his new family.

In his mind he heard a refrain: I had to return to the Balkans, I did not have to return to the Balkans! Over the years, this refrain burrowed ever deeper into the depths of his quietude.

During those long conversations with Mr. K., and with him alone, the tranquility in my father's soul could be stirred, releasing those long-buried days in Constantinople. He was surrounded by his books—those silent but living witnesses to his turbulent times in that imperial city.

Here were the books he had bought from the sellers of used books, whose stalls lined the courtyards of the University of Constantinople. Hearing my father speak of them, Mr. K. would, in turn, recall the many bookstalls of Paris along the quays of the Seine.

My father's illusions of Constantinople ended in this pile of books that he kept with him throughout his life, and they remained a great family resource, a hidden signpost for us through surge upon surge of Balkan storms that divided nations and led to ruinous, fratricidal civil wars.

The books became sacred objects for Father, Mother, and us children, wherever our Balkan fate led us. Those days in Constantinople, however, rested with my father, and he alone could revive, interpret, and prolong them.

In among the books that he had carried home from his great journey, there, bright like an eye wide open, rested the peacock-shaped radio with its feathers fanned out.

Late, late at night he received Constantinople clearly on the radio, and he would be transported by the movements of Eastern ritual tugging him yet further away beyond Constantinople to the gates of the Levant, to Cairo, to those places he had reached in his youth.

Mr. K. had carried back in his books from the West his own bundle of illusions, which, in those postwar years when the idea of Socialism was first realized, could easily have embittered his life. But no one could diminish his great love for books. He, too, had gathered in his books an era he was not able to live, a time he had to transplant back in the

Balkans. A former doctoral student at the Sorbonne, a participant in the Spanish Civil War on the side of La Pasionaria, he trusted only in his books during those chaotic years in the Balkans. He turned to his books during every misunderstanding he had with his own times. And for a time he remained, if not redeemed, comforted.

My father somehow kept his Eastern dream, retained in the reservoir of his books, turned inward. He kept it inside and so had little quarrel with the people of his own time. His Eastern dream was his escape, as much a part of his life as death.

Unlike my father, Mr. K. turned his Western dream outward, toward others; he wanted to influence those around him, and, needless to say, he was misunderstood. He found his greatest comfort in his love of books, a love he shared with my father. My father, in turn, had no other friend than Mr. K. in whom to confide the secrets of his library.

As a result, their friendship thrived.

Friends

*T*oward the end of his life, my father had many books but few friends. In his youth he had had many friends but few books.

Most often, it was books that led to friendship; more rarely, friendship to books. Mr. K. was the rarer type of friend. He had studied in Paris in his youth, my father in Constantinople—my father during the collapse of the Ottoman Empire and the dawn of the era of Atatürk, old Mr. K. during the time of Europe's descent into Fascism.

Both were captives of an eternal dream, my father of an Eastern dream, Mr. K. of a Western one. They maintained their friendship through frequent exchange of their dreams, dreams that merged with one another.

In this way they sustained their friendship.

In the twilight of their lives, when Stalinism was still the law in this part of the Balkans, the regime kept the two of them, the one with his Eastern illusions, the other with his Western ones, somewhat, yet not entirely, on the fringes; they could still be of use for some purpose or other. Because they remained "unsuitable" for the party, they had greater maneuvering room in their private lives. The fact that the regime held them both at a distance allowed a secret and unobserved friendship to flourish between them.

They were both polyglots, yet as the years passed, they both had trouble coping with Macedonian, especially my father.

In his fervent zeal as a bibliophile, old Mr. K. had also acquired some manuscripts in Ottoman script. He impatiently waited for my father to interpret these texts, and then, so they could publish their joint translations, he would seek out potential publishers, which he never found. He did finally manage to reach an agreement with a medical journal in the city for a translation of some old notes about Macedonian medicinal herbs.

Their joint translation resembled an extraordinary act of haggling in both languages, an unparalleled and arduous linguistic battle in which the ultimate goal, their success, had to be sensed in the aroma of the herbs from the original text that lingered in their translation.

They spent exhausting nights together, entering linguistic warrens, certain they knew the exit when, in fact, they were being led into greater linguistic uncertainty.

At last, their translations were published!

They were as happy as children and clearly filled with tremendous pride that their friendship had endured translation.

Autodidacts

*H*aving left the Balkans in their youth, one to Constantinople, the other to Paris, they had many passions, like all young people, but it was their love of books that remained most engraved upon them. Although they had both studied at great universities, one at the University of Constantinople, the other at the Sorbonne, they both still had much to learn; they remained great autodidacts, and they remained forever fascinated by how time gathered in libraries, in religious buildings, in bridges.

But, in their impoverished Balkans, nothing remained eternal—no bridge, no place of worship, no library. In their restless Balkans it was their books that could be carried along, that could endure, that could come to life. They believed that the fullness of life, which they themselves forever lacked, rested in their books.

The people in the Balkans never had the opportunity to heal themselves: just as one war ended, another war approached. Just when they became accustomed to communicating in one language, another came along. It was a hellish situation. People viewed our father and Mr. K., with their books, as some sort of outdated missionaries, as men with a different turn of mind; no one could understand their great love of books.

Those confounded books were a source of understanding or misunderstanding. My father and Mr. K. believed that people would understand them and would accept their love of books.

Each worked his own library, his own little part of the world, his Garden of Eden. At the same time, they built their own small Towers of Babel with secret walls made of those books that fate had assigned to them at that first turn, at all turns. The uncertainty that they might not fully succeed in shaping their libraries ate away at them.

These self-taught men, these Don Quixotes of the Balkans, came here at the wrong time. They had great and tender hearts; they had within them the heart of all books.

Libraries

After Mr. K. and my father had exhausted the major political questions they had learned about from listening to both Western and Eastern radio stations, they would usually end up talking about the pains, along with the pleasures, that they derived from their books.

Mr. K. was consumed by the idea of having as many books as possible; he wanted to own every book in the world. My father wanted to have those genuine books, those books that gave his life direction, and that he could read and reread as long as he lived.

Mr. K. wanted a veritable jungle of books into which he could enter and lose himself, in which he could spend his whole life. My father, however, wanted a forest, a garden in which each flower would smile at him when he wished to pick it.

Mr. K. frequently brought over books that would be of great interest to my father but of secondary interest to himself. My father read them and then conscientiously returned them to Mr. K.; my father, enthused by the contents of the book, would set off on a quest for new books.

Mr. K. frequently brought my father books worthy of translation, hoping to find an occupation for the two of them during those years of poverty.

Mr. K. had converted nearly half of his house into a library. An entire room was filled with rows of bookcases, like in a public library, just as he had seen in his travels in Paris. One had to admit that in our city there was not yet, nor would there be for a long time, a library as big, as rich, and as beautiful as his.

Mr. K. often told my father that he dreamed of converting the entire house into a library.

A Boarder in Babel

Mr. K. always came to visit my father either very late or very early in the day. He always arrived with a new book, a new document, a map; it was as if he pulled books out of his very self, from out of his body, from out of thin air. In his hands he always held the first book he wanted to show my father.

Absorbed with the books, he did not pay attention to anyone until he entered my father's library. He would begin by telling my father of some great discovery, as if he had found some valuable manuscript from the lost continent of Atlantis.

When he worked at the university, he would search with his students for any books and forgotten documents in their houses. When he left the university, his faithful students continued to bring him old, yellowed documents their parents no longer wished to keep. Until his retirement he was allowed to work in the Institute of Folklore. He was given a small office, located above the other rooms, a space under the roof between two sloping walls that had been partitioned off just for him—a hanging bower of Babel. When someone entered this little room, someone who did not know how to get through, books and papers fell every which way. Someone once told him that his books would squeeze him out of the room, and he replied that such was his ideal, his ultimate dream.

A new book was an occasion for which Mr. K. could interrupt my father's work without upsetting him. Once my father was interrupted, it was difficult for him to return to the thought that had occurred to him while reading.

Mr. K. often whispered to my father his predictions about where danger would come from next. Their mutual love of books, unique in our city, had created tremendous trust between them.

Long into the night, while they worked out their daily strategy for the survival of their families, they would discover which way the wind was blowing.

At night, Mr. K. usually listened to and interpreted the news on the Western radio stations, while my father listened to the Eastern ones. On through the night until dawn they pieced together the truth from the two sources they had reached independently.

The books gave them the strength to wait fully prepared for any new capricious blows of that Balkan fate that could come from anywhere at any moment. Yes, the books guided their lives, and they themselves had to adapt so as not to end up as misunderstood Balkan Don Quixotes, as Bouvard and Pécuchet.

Language Quarrels

When my father and Mr. K. could not find just the right word while translating, they swore at both languages and recalled the curse of Babel, that source of imperfection in the order of human affairs. They would find fault with everyone. Then, disrupting the usual quiet in which their ideas most often took flight, Father and Mr. K. would fall into endless quarrels about grammar.

My father calmly brought forth his arguments and proposed various solutions.

Mr. K. was absolutely categorical in his knowledge of his language. It always had to be his way and no other!

Each insisted on his tremendous knowledge of his own language. My father boasted of his knowledge of the language they were translating from, Mr. K. of the language they were translating into.

When their linguistic quarrel reached its climax, my mother would come into the study carrying a tray, most often with sweet fruit preserves and coffee or tea.

Mother, poor thing, could not understand how there could be such a fight over a single word. Really, weren't there other words in the language? she would mutter to herself as she left the old men, who had calmed down but who were ready at any moment to start fighting over some new word.

When, late at night, exhausted, they would complete their translating for the day, though satisfied with the work completed, they would also be anxious to continue on into the night, under the glow of the lamps, their ongoing debate about languages and the curse of Babel.

My father most often maintained that the solution to Babel was to be found in continuous translation, as if he were imagining the task of the happy Balkan Sisyphus—Mr. K., who thought that salvation would be found in a single common language. As a young man in Paris Mr. K. had followed the great European debates over the introduction of Esperanto as a universal language. He had remained forever captive to the idea of a single language, even an artificial one, that could unite the world.

My father was prepared to accept Mr. K.'s opinion that there should be one language, especially after their great, nearly insurmountable difficulties during their translation work, but he would not agree that this language could be an artificial one such as Esperanto or another such language.

My father maintained that such a universal language could only be a natural language with hundreds or thousands of years of existence, with all the mechanisms for resistance and defense, even if this language were spoken by only a small group of people. He was certainly thinking as well about the small languages of the Balkans, which now breathed freely but which could be smothered by an artificial language.

Mr. K. did not agree but continued with his arguments until later, much later into the night.

Balkan Babel

During dark and troubled times, my father often trusted in his books when he could not trust in people.

My mother often heard his whispering over the pages of an opened book. At first, she worried that my father would not return from his books, but in time she got used to it and understood Father's behavior when books were at issue.

My mother rarely interrupted my father while he was reading; by mutual agreement she did so only when they needed to discuss some curve in the road of life that their children confronted.

My father hoped most of all that his heirs, we children, would study and become doctors so we would always be of use to people or, for the same reason, that we would become engineers, but in all his children he constantly instilled his love of studying languages. We should study the languages of our people, the languages of those both near to us and far away . . .

When there was a question about the children's schooling, my father would exchange a word or two only with Mr. K., who had studied pedagogy in Paris at the Sorbonne. They always reached agreement. Even though Mr. K. still believed that the time would come when the world would have a single language, until then one had to learn the languages of those nearby, our neighbors.

Mr. K. once told my father that the Balkans were cursed, that they were a small Tower of Babel, a Balkan Babel, but that people in the Balkans could save themselves if they reached agreement, if they united and joined together through all their languages. Here my father and Mr. K. reached complete agreement and gave direction to their children's lives.

A Choice

$\mathcal{M}$y father and Mr. K. often spoke about the arrangement of the books in their respective libraries.

Mr. K. was the first to construct library shelves in his library with rows of bookcases, some of wood and others of metal. First he created the space, and then he filled it with books. He of course arranged the books according to their content, by the subject matter that interested him.

My father had, in fact, a smaller space for his books. In addition to the cabinets, he had a small, functional library in his study, where he also kept his dictionaries, encyclopedias, and grammars. The books were usually placed in the order in which he intended to read them. Once the books were read, he always returned them to their original location. Thus he was completing a circle made up of the books he had read, which was also the circle of his life. The circle was of course never completed.

My father knew that every selection of a book, no matter how perfect, could limit him, could take away other possibilities.

Mr. K. often complained to my father during their inexhaustible conversations that it was impossible to remember every book in his library. For my father, it was critical to determine which books to consign to oblivion. Aside from an acceptance of death, a concept he owed to his reading of the essays of Montaigne, the proper selection of books was the most significant principle of his life.

My father told Mr. K. that one's library was like one's fate. Even if one cannot avoid one's fate, one can avoid unnecessary books. But which are those? asked Mr. K. thoughtfully.

The books remained silent witnesses to the time my father and Mr. K. spent together. They had intended to read through all the books of both of their libraries. Later on, they abandoned this idea so they could dedicate themselves to translating works from languages that they did not know very well. Here, too, they were disheartened because their translations were rarely published, almost never, in fact. Something was always found lacking in them, yet others made use of them later on. They finally decided to compile, using the books they owned and those they would acquire later on, a type of catalogue of the major Balkan ideas of their time. Because of this idea their lives were engulfed in the unpredictable currents of Balkan history.

Sacrifice
for Books

$\mathcal{M}$y father had friends who would have sacrificed their lives for their books and indeed many who did so. All these friends were bound by an invisible thread that emerged from the manuscripts and gave significance to their lives.

It could easily be stated that Mr. K., my father's friend, had the largest private library in our city. He faithfully spent his whole life constructing his Babel of books in the hope that one day he would be enthroned within it and could then read all the books in the order he had taken his whole life to form.

Mr. K. was an obvious casualty, as are many true bibliophiles, so rare in the Balkans, of possessing a greater number of books than was humanly possible to read in one lifetime. Unable to comprehend his era, he lived consumed by this contradiction. His eyesight grew ever weaker. Finally, only a certain internationally renowned ophthalmologist in Paris could save his sight. With his social insurance, to which he regularly contributed, and some old savings, he gathered together sufficient funds and set off for Paris.

The dream he believed had vanished forever came to life.

Paris unfolded before him untouched since the time of his youth, when, spellbound, he had made it his own.

First he went to the quays along the Seine, as if along banks of books, so he could resume his never-ending conversations with the clever secondhand booksellers of Paris, those faithful keepers of the books and their eternity.

He recognized some of the old booksellers and became acquainted with their successors. Much time had flowed under the bridges on the Seine. He found his way with ease through the land of the Paris booksellers; he felt right at home while he discovered new books, maps, engravings, medals, herbaria, insect collections, a variety of maps of the Balkans. He recognized his quarter in the Parisian bookish Babylon. He was in his own personal heaven. He was happy here in this library by the two fraternal tributaries of the one large river with its infinite branches in time.

In the evenings, when the eye of the sun cast a final glance on the last of the Paris bridges, he returned from the land of the Paris booksellers.

Sometimes the booksellers would detain him late at night to end the evening in a Paris bistro in fervent conversations about books; they considered him a worthy returnee from some sort of distant exile.

He would return late at night to his hotel, his little suitcase stuffed with books, those he had bought and others that had been presented to him, gifts from the Paris booksellers, who valued Mr. K. as a rare and worthy lover of books, one among the race of great European readers. Then my father's friend Mr. K. forgot what time of his life he was in and gave himself over to the time of books.

Late into the night, with the last light of his remaining vision, Mr. K. paged through and examined the books he was given. He lived in his dream of books.

As soon as the new day dawned, he traced the same circle along the shores of the Seine, with its new books and the fidelity of its booksellers. And so it continued to the end of this little holiday in his life, in the movable feast of Paris.

Mr. K. completely forgot about the eye operation for which he had come to Paris. Starting in the early morning hours, always wanting to overtake the great throngs of the Paris crowds, he would find himself along the Seine with its chain of wondrous bridges and the endless books that gleamed for him like pearls, in that space where he believed life was returning to him. Mr. K. reestablished his order in this time he believed was his alone because only he understood its significance.

Mr. K., so mesmerized by the books, nearly forgot to eat. He ate one meal a day, French bread with pâté, which he chewed absentmindedly, engrossed in some new and unfamiliar book, which he now wanted to own. It was the same every day to the end of his Paris eternity.

One morning, after the funds that had been set aside for the operation by the famous Parisian ophthalmologist had melted away in book purchases, Mr. K.'s helpful Parisian friend—the one who had earlier corresponded with him about the operation—came to tell him, before he went off to the bookstalls, that the date had been set for his eye operation.

Mr. K. did not say a word; he just led his Parisian friend to his room in the Paris hotel.

Mr. K. tried to open the door. They finally managed to get the door open. First Mr. K. went in, then his friend.

And what should his friend see there?

The books that filled nearly every inch of space in the room spoke for themselves. They answered all the questions that needed to be put to Mr. K.

The next day, at dawn, before the streets were filled with the usual Paris crowds, there making its way toward the Paris railroad station, the Gare de Lyon, from which trains left for the Balkans, was a small van over-stuffed with new Parisian books bought by Mr. K., who, though now nearly blind but satisfied with his remaining light, looked, surely for the last time, out at the Paris quays along the Seine. He was content with some sort of victory whose meaning he alone understood.

The End of Time

To Prof. ANTON POLANSHCHAK

It seems that the people who build libraries throughout their lives die twice: most often their libraries die with them.

Marcel Proust

*I*n discovering the works of Marcel Proust in the Balkans, Professor Polanshchak actually discovered the richness of reading in his own life.

The novels of Proust that make up the cycle *In Search of Lost Time* occupied the central place in his library, which took up the entire wall space in his house.

He spent a great deal of thought on the arrangement of his books. His order made the books alive, ready to radiate their energy. Among the books, in what constituted at the same time a sepulchre of his era, of his time, one's attention was drawn to the skull of a former Roman legionnaire that had been exhumed somewhere in the very heart of the Balkans.

The skull was nearly decomposed with age, but it had miraculously preserved its teeth securely in place, and in among them shone two new crowns, alongside other teeth sporting new fillings. Professor Polanshchak's library told the most about his life. He had dedicated his life to the reading and interpretation of the works of Marcel Proust. If Proust had discovered his past time, his childhood, and his youth in the eternity of art in the heart of Cartesian and Bergsonian Europe, Professor Polanshchak wanted to arrive at this same discovery in the Balkans. The skull, with its filled teeth, grotesque and bizarre, was witness to times lost and times found in his Balkans.

The Books in One's Life

To OLGA NICHOTA, *professor of the French language*

When the people who had most frequently surrounded her became scarce in her life, perhaps due mainly to old age, Professor Nichota increasingly abandoned herself and her trust to books. She secretly wished that her life would be extinguished while she was reading a book. In our city there was no greater reader than she was. In her youth before the war she had been the first to complete her French degree in a high school in Salonika, and at this time a great and genuine love of literature took root in her, a love that lasted until her death. To the end of her life, after the war and during the Stalinist era, during the Balkan migrations, she remained faithful to her notes and several French books. During troubled times in the Balkans she was radiant in her knowledge, sensibility, and goodness. Generations owed their successful path in life most of all to this quiet, wise old woman, with her eternally youthful air. Yes, in the city there was no greater reader than she was. I, more than any other student, brought her new books to read from various sources, but most often from my father's library.

The news of her death sadly passed me by in the senseless bustle of life; the last book she requested has remained with me forever. There was in her wide soul great power—acquired through her constant and thoughtful reading—that tamed her fear of death. In her sparely furnished study it was as if some quiet solitude shone there, and the shadow of her soul turned the pages of her abandoned books.

Books were the true bridges that connected her with others and with the world. When the day came when she felt that she was reading the last book of her life, she used her final strength to clean up and put her house in order, then she gathered up the books that needed to be returned. The last day of her life was like all the others. The same peacefulness reigned. Just the turning of the final pages of the book . . . Everything was completed and ready for the sad ceremony at which she would not be present. Gide's *Strait Is the Gate* was placed beside her hands.

In the final years of her life she often read scientific journals in the fields of medicine and astronomy, but she remained faithful to her grammars, dictionaries, and encyclopedias. In her study, which began to fade away after she was gone, were left behind the last books we had lent her, with individual notes for each one of us, arranged in ways that could be taken as her last requests. In this way each book bore witness as a unique sign whose complete understanding was impossible without our interpretation and that must have represented, according to her religious idea, a bridge between her spiritual eternity and those of us who remained behind in this life.

On her desk, under a gold wall clock and beside the little blue vase that always held a fresh flower, all her dictionaries from various times and in various languages were stacked one on top of another in the form of a pyramid. The tip of the pyramid was a miniature dictionary, the final point of all her books like the narrow way to the other world.

Father's Books,
Migrations, Stalinism,
the Balkan Wall

The Spyglass

Sometime in the 1920s, my father brought home an old spyglass that he had bought in a secondhand store in the Grand Bazaar in Constantinople. The store mainly sold old war trophies and other objects from the Ottoman period. The spyglass had belonged to a Turkish Janissary commander. This information was clearly engraved on it. In the secondhand store there were various other odds and ends, but it was mainly the trophies and weapons that caught one's eye. Here sparkled a Janissary chain, worn by the most elite of the Ottoman military corps to demonstrate their membership. Over there one's eye was struck by the glint of broad, curved Janissary swords; by a small Janissary flag next to a bow and arrow; by Janissary flintlock rifles, Janissary cauldrons and spoons—all the particular symbols of that old military order. Although the Janissary era—dating from the time of the Ottoman period's grandeur and decline—was long over, many people stopped in at the Constantinople secondhand shop where Janissary relics were bought and sold. The time of the Janissaries did not pass away easily. It had remained within the people.

Father looked with indifference at the Janissary trophies. His gaze rested with excitement only on this large spyglass. He himself could not explain why he had bought the Janissary spyglass and brought it home to the Balkans.

Those close to my father found it strange when they saw him back in his own country with the spyglass. They imagined that he stared across the border at the opposite shore of the lake and contemplated his future journey. Grandfather was the one most pleased by the spyglass. It was as if he had been condemned to live a solitary life by the shore of the lake. All his kin had crossed the border, first his brothers and sisters, then his sons and daughters from his first marriage. When he saw his oldest son from his second marriage return from Constantinople with the large spyglass in hand, he couldn't have been happier. He had thought that if anyone had been destined to remain abroad, it would be this son. Grandfather, with childish glee, was delighted both with his son's return and with the spyglass. He kept it with him day and night.

At the break of day he would make his way to the edge of the lake. When the air was most transparent, he could look through the spyglass to the opposite shore of the lake, across the border. He walked along the shore looking through the spyglass. While thus sailing in place, he imagined himself the captain of a vanished ship.

Many years have passed since then. Grandfather vanished in a splendid dream with the spyglass in his hand. A long time thereafter, the spyglass was virtually forgotten, as if it had been exhausted from use. The spyglass would have remained forgotten had my father not taken it out one day and made the fateful decision that we would all cross the border in the old family rowboat and remain forever outcasts.

We traveled at night. We could not cross the border in daylight without being seen or being stopped, even without border guards on either side of the lake. The border changed so quickly that the border guards could not arrive fast enough to protect it.

After that long night of uncertainty, when our closest companion was fear, the first rays of the sun splashed down. We were far enough from our native shore. We could not have foreseen that we would never return. While Father, with his family close beside him, was unable to uproot his family hearth, Mother, deep inside, secretly held out the hope of return.

After many years my father held the spyglass in his hands for the first time since that moment he brought it from Constantinople. He pulled out all three extensions, he stood at the helm, and he began to look around. First he turned the spyglass toward the Albanian shore and looked for his own house, where he had left his mother by his not-yet-uprooted hearth.

He looked steadfastly toward his house, toward the garden. As he whispered something, a few droplets dampened his face. One could not tell whether these were from the waves that struck the side of the boat or whether Father was crying for the first time in his life.

He said something quietly to himself. We could not understand what it was. The only thing we could imagine was that he had reached some understanding with his now distant mother. Then he turned the spyglass toward the monastery perched on the mountaintop above the town, where members of our family would go regardless of their faith. He kept the spyglass trained on the monastery for a long time. Then he whispered some words that will remain forever unknown.

Through the Constantinople spyglass my father peered at places in the life he had once led, at a life that he alone doubted would ever return. At one point he aimed the spyglass toward the sky. A droplet clearly slid down the shaft of the spyglass. Father looked through the lens of the spyglass, which seemed to hold the gaze of his own father, who had departed long ago. Now the son, with spyglass in hand, moved beyond his father. He felt as if he had broken some sort of promise. Along the side of the spyglass another drop ran down.

Now that we had crossed the first border in our lives, it was time for my father to turn the spyglass toward the nearer shore, toward the harbor of our first exile. First he rested his sight on the river that springs from the lake and later empties into the big sea.

The family rowboat arrived at the very point where the river leaves the lake, by the first bridge. It was as if we were now following the path of the eels that made their way up to this river from the sea and that, though depleted in number and hunted, still managed to survive and make their way back out toward the sea, traveling as far as the great ocean. Secretly, we children thought that we would follow the same path. Father believed it, too. After all, had he not once said that all roads were open once you left your native hearth?

Many years passed, and we still remained nestled in the town by the river that flows out of the lake. My father's thoughts did not stop here;

they traveled ever forward, crossing new borders, stopping beside other rivers. My father's thoughts continued on to where the rivers flowed out, my mother's thoughts to where the rivers began.

When the Great War ended, my father did not return to his birthplace, an hour away by rowboat, but set off toward another river. We abandoned the route of the eels because it was impossible to follow them. Our great dream was now cut off. The border we had crossed became even more tightly closed; only the eels continued to traverse it unobstructed. At a time when the Balkans were the most closed in, as if in a large cage, each small country its own smaller cage, we continued to think of the eels' route out to the ocean and across to America, returning with each generation. How unlucky people are . . .

Our route to a different river carried a different fate. We stopped in a house by a river, near a wooden bridge. The river gushed from a mountain with high white summits, and after crossing yet another Balkan border, it flowed down into the nearby southern sea. We nearly forgot about the spyglass. Even without it, one could clearly see the opposite shore of this river, above which one could glimpse the old fortress built during the Ottoman era.

We stayed a long time in the house by the rapid river. We nearly forgot about the pathway of the eels, about the myth that they follow the river out to the ocean and travel on to America. Time passed, as did Father's dream of our departure either to the West or to the East. The borders of all our possible exits were closed, several of them nailed tightly shut. The border that we had crossed ended up as one of the most tightly closed in the world. Even news of deaths coming from both sides seemed to stop at the very border. Accursed times . . .

As we children grew older, our memories of the lake grew stronger. One day, we asked for the first time whether we might go there, nearer to the border, nearer to our people. Just before we left, we remembered Father's spyglass. He kept it by his books. He gave it to us. But it was as if he wanted to tell us that there was no longer anything to be seen.

We set off in the direction of the lake. We came nearer to the border by the side of the monastery. My older brothers remembered it from when we first saw it from the other side of the border, from our home-town. The monastery rose from a large outcropping overlooking the lake. Below, across the border, along the shore, white houses were strung as if on a necklace. One among them had to be ours, the one taken from us, the source of all our dreams. And now the spyglass, the old Ottoman spyglass, which had not yet discharged its duty, was called upon to serve as the only bridge that could shorten the distance and bring us closer to our family home.

The spyglass was the only large eye that could masterfully cross that border so vigilantly guarded on both sides.

We each took turns gazing through the spyglass at our little town, the impossible goal of our return. It seemed as if the inhabitants of two different planets had quarreled, not people close to each other, many even from the same families.

We returned home with the spyglass. We placed it once again among Father's books. Our father, unlike us children, never went up to the heights by the monastery to see our native country, our house . . .

Many, many more years passed.

Miraculously, the border opened. Anyone could cross it.

The spyglass remained forgotten among Father's books.

The Globe

*I*n the middle of Father's books was a section with old charts and maps as well as drawings made by famous travel writers from Europe or Asia who had traveled through the Balkans.

There were various systems for notating cartographic information. Here jumbled together were alphabets, faiths, planned itineraries, all left behind on the maps to maintain people's illusions of former glory. There was also a relief map of the Balkans, made a long time ago according to the ideas of a self-taught cartographer.

The unevenness of my father's soul was inscribed in the relief, and someone looking at it could examine, in the region of interest to him, all the vivid impressions that area had made on the eyes of that anonymous mapmaker.

On a great globe Father had corrected, added, and removed some of the area representing his native land on the relief map made by that anonymous author—a bit of lake, a bit of mountain and valley, a monastery on a hilltop. He kept some parts, added some others, making changes according to the narratives of the old Eastern and Western travelogues.

My father remained virtually chained down in the Balkans after the two trips he had made in his youth at the beginning of the twentieth century, one to the East, to Constantinople and Cairo, the other to the West, to Rome and Venice.

He remained in his own personal Tower of Babel, which overflowed with books in various languages and alphabets, to prepare for his great voyage, a continuation of his exile. But he did not have much luck with his Balkan fate. Events were settled here with more difficulty than elsewhere.

When he found a way out of the ruins of the Ottoman Empire and broke his faith with the labyrinthine Constantinople of his mother's identity, my father set off toward his father's country and toward his Albanian identity. There he came up against Fascism. Fleeing from it, he came to another country, a different fate. Paradoxically, or however one views it, during the Stalinist period, although caged in, he experienced a time in which his family could peacefully develop. For the first time he was happy, truly happy, the happy Sisyphus with his family. He knew that in the Balkans, luck does not last long, so he constantly prepared for some new voyage.

Stalinism shut all my father's illusions into a cage, but, through his books, which rescued him at every phase of his great exile as he passed from the ruins of one empire into the labyrinth of this new ideology, he found his true exit.

My father never traveled to the North on the Balkan Express or to the East on the Venice–Simplon Orient. As a result, as he sat among his salvaged books in his Babel room, no one hindered him from contemplating and carrying out his journeys.

Among the maps, the hand-drawn maps, and the relief maps of the Balkans, Father had a globe that he had brought from Constantinople, made at the beginning of the century, when the Ottoman Empire still existed. My father penned corrections on this globe, adding and subtracting as history demanded.

Sometimes in the middle of the night or just at dawn he would get up and turn the globe, rummaging among his books to find the clearest magnifying glass with the best magnification; this, in turn, would awaken my mother from the light sleep that allowed her to protect Father's deep sleep and all her children. At such times she would whisper, mostly to herself: *That one*—that's how she sometimes referred to him, especially when she had some long-simmering anger layered in the depths of her soul—*he is thinking once again about some impossible voyage! That poor man! Once again he is going to waste everything, especially his sight. He will torment that globe, the planet of his illusions. But there will be no escape, and that will be the end of it! No one has left the Stalinist Balkan cage alive. His mind will deceive him for no purpose.*

Through the night Father continued to ponder that quixotic heroic voyage that would never be realized in the closed expanse of his time. In vain he spun the globe faster and faster; its supporting axis was like the custodian of the entire weight of the earth's rivers, oceans, and mountains.

Unable in his lifetime to carry out a longer and more lasting sojourn away from the Balkans, one he could have contemplated, imagined, and sketched out, at least on his globe, my father, struggling powerlessly in his Stalinist cage, would seek his unfinished travels in his dreams, dreams that grew stronger in his imagination through intense reading of old European travel diaries, particularly those in French. He would awaken at some point during the night and jot down his dream travels onto the globe, then give it a spin. And so the subconscious illusion of a finished journey was made complete.

What Father sought in his books and wanted to sketch out on the maps and finally on the globe was the inaccessible line of identity of his family's predecessors in the Balkans. He wanted to impose on the globe a dimension it could not naturally have: one that would attest to the paths of identity going deep, deep back in time. He was well acquainted with the Ottoman Empire in the Balkans. He had penetrated the secrets of the legal organization of the empire during the time of its fall, when an entire system of laws, moral obligations, and traditions that had constituted the archetypal core of nearly all the Balkan peoples had ceased to be valid. My father's life in the Balkans was a string of paradoxical situations that saved him more often than not but that also led him and his family into new uncertainties. He had to seize the salvation of his family even from defeats.

After he discovered three centuries' worth of old court records from the *qadi*, or judge, of Bitola, city of consuls, he believed that he had found the crowning arguments that would allow the Balkan nations, freed at last from Ottoman rule, to rise above their cursed divisions. He knew that many secrets, great and small, of every Balkan family would lie hidden in the massive Balkan temporal magma, which would always retain its vital significance. He wanted to delve as deep as possible into his family's past in the long Ottoman period, to draw out as much illumination as possible from the yellowing documents beside his ever-burning golden lamp.

He descended deep, as far down as the eighteenth century, into the history of his family, following his mother's line. He discovered an old qadi family but failed to sort out the subsequent details concerning the loss of his mother's identity, the arrival of his ancestors in the Balkans, how the family branched out, and how, moreover, it remained always faithful to the qadi tradition. He could not figure out what fateful impulse had led them to travel to Constantinople before the fall of the Ottoman Empire and to involve themselves in the battles for position in a state that was tossing like a ship in the midst of a storm. After discovering the qadi documents, he knew more than ever before that he would be settling scores with the Ottoman period until the end of his life and that many secrets would remain to be unraveled by his heirs. It could not be otherwise.

In these moments of haziness and hopelessness my father would unconsciously spin the globe, and it would transport him in an instant to new and unknown regions, to other continents, where there were surely some of his kin. They were scattered across the globe even where thought itself could not reach.

He turned the old globe and looked through older documents. He tried to imagine his maternal ancestor, the old qadi, perhaps the author of one of these documents. Before departing forever for Constantinople, he might have come to the lake one last time with his large family to spend his last Balkan summer there, to have something to remember in faraway Anatolia.

The qadi had become close with our grandfather's family and had even become the blood brother of some of them. Wishing to maintain ties with the land he would be leaving forever, he gave his consent for

71

his youngest daughter to become the wife of our grandfather, who was already a widower. Then he left for Turkey, never to return. There he built his family. Later, Turkey itself became too small for them, and his descendants spread out over the globe. Many close relatives, even first cousins, were forgotten forever. Only chance could bring them together. The qadi never saw his youngest daughter again. He passed from this world with a gaping wound in his soul. He left her a small inheritance, money in an Ottoman bank in Constantinople, of which all trace was lost. In the thirties she would go for the first time to Constantinople, to İzmir, and to other cities where her people had gone. They were all lawyers. They remembered my father, her son, because he had studied to be a lawyer in Constantinople. He left them, when no one believed he would, particularly after his meeting with Atatürk, when, had he remained, all doors in Turkey would have been thrown wide open to him. And those doors were large. How could anyone else fathom it, when he could not comprehend it himself. His mother set off to accomplish what her son had not been able to: to make it possible for them to settle in Turkey. But, she returned to the Balkans with a heavy heart, feeling abandoned and forgotten. Her first cousins ridiculed her archaic Turkish. They said they were amused by how their cousin from Albania spoke. Grandmother eventually left Turkey without truly understanding which country was her fatherland. She returned to the Balkans just as her son was preparing his departure from his own fatherland. Not a long time passed before his mother died with bitterness in her soul.

And so it was that my father never ceased contemplating which path he should follow, which migration he should join. He had forgotten that he was already enclosed in this Balkan cage and that his illusory plans for continuing his great migration could no longer be realized. But no one could prevent him from traveling in his thoughts. And oh, how he traveled!

His thoughts turned once more to his mother's last trip to Turkey. Deep down he was satisfied that his mother had finally made peace with the impulse that had made his return to the Balkans inevitable. My father had returned to the old house by the lake. In the doorway of the family house stood *his* father, who had grown frail with worry but who now became a bit livelier knowing he had lived to see the return of his son from Constantinople, something that everyone had told him would never come to pass. But he had always stubbornly believed it. He died soon after, lucky, one might say, because his son was there to take over the family. Afterward much Balkan history weighed on my father's shoulders. Sensing that Fascism could overtake him, he saved himself by crossing the border with his family and in so doing met up with Communism.

Was this fate's revenge on him for abandoning Constantinople and not planting his family in peaceful realms of existence far from this Balkan hell? In those moments when he could not discern the truth he spun the globe, and his gaze turned to the only large family photograph in which he appeared together with both his father, whose large, sunken eyes emphasized his constant melancholy, and his mother with the energetic gaze she always had in life.

Father's gaze rested on his mother, and it seemed as if he could detect a change in the photograph. Her sweet vigor had weakened; her longing for her family had weakened. And there, standing upright in the photograph above his parents, was my father, in the bloom of youth, just returned from Constantinople, wearing an energetic expression and a sharpened moustache, like those sported by the Young Turks ready to hasten the end of the Ottoman Empire . . .

Father reflected, sitting beside the globe that spun before his eyes, beside his opened books, maps, and geographic charts, and, along who knows what path, he asked himself whether he had set out along the correct path, whether he had betrayed his fate.

What if? . . . What if? . . . What if? . . .

He thought and thought, rearranging his thoughts.

Did it make sense to fight against an unforeseeable outcome and slip into fatalism?

Would it have been better to have followed the path of his mother's

or his father's identity, or should he have chosen some middle path—
the exile of his large family? . . .

But what had Father chosen?

What path had he followed?

What path would his heirs continue along?

Yet another night overtook him, and he was far from finding a true answer, if such an answer existed at all. When he was certain that there was no answer to be found nor any new course of migration, he consoled himself by spinning the globe.

The Family Clock

*I*n all our wanderings, eluding expected wars and occupations, always with our books—if not all of them, then always, without fail, the holy ones—as well as the bunch of keys to our abandoned houses, their locks empty of all hope of return, we always took with us the old family pendulum clock, inherited from who knows which ancestors, the clock of all our times.

When we set off, we took the clock with us, as if in carrying it we carried all our times. When we would arrive at either our temporary or our final destination of resettlement, before anything else we checked to see whether time still passed through our clock. At times we wondered how the clock's old, rusted mechanism was able to budge after we wound it with the old key, which was rusted as well.

We kept the clock in constant motion, like a living member of the family. And when at each hour the clock marked the time in its raspy old voice, its chime always struck a different chord in us. We listened to its sound, which seemed to us like the muffled voice of some unknown ancestor.

The old clock held a sacrosanct place in the family iconography even after we crossed the border for good. It stayed with us, one of the rare family objects that bore witness to our abandoned and later confiscated house. It seemed as if the most important messages from the family's life by the lake were conveyed to us through the life of our wound-up clock.

Inside the clock, during one of the rare moments when it was opened, my father found a yellowed slip of paper folded and refolded several times. Now what in the world could this be? My father was quite excited as he carefully unfolded it, carefully, lest the paper disintegrate and the message disappear. My father easily recognized the archaic Arabic script. In a moment he had confirmed that on the paper, now fully spread out, was written a perpetual calendar. The directions, written by some unknown ancestor, were calculated by Eastern rather than Western time. There were also several accounts about the origin of the clock and its previous owners.

After he had fully examined its contents, my father carefully folded up the note and returned it to its former place, because it too could be considered an integral part of the clock's mechanism. It contributed to the precise telling of time.

And so the clock remained a faithful guardian of the time stolen from us on the other side of the border, taken away irrevocably. Our lives, many near their end, were the greatest evidence of this. The clock was also a faithful guardian of our family history. Sometimes this old clock, with its simple mechanism, appeared to us a skeleton of time, and often, with its slow pulse at every beat, it was a source of fear, a curve of unexpected fate.

Not only did it faithfully measure time during those years of difficult exile, it also calmed us to face our future, it softened the strikes of time, it was on our side. In time the big family clock received its worthy place in Father's library, just below the holy books . . .

The large family clock sitting among Father's books seemed to give a rhythm to the many-faceted quiet that was disrupted by the constant turning of pages. It was not possible for the clock to stop ticking; it was not possible for the clock to remain unwound. A near-religious attention was devoted to keeping the clock from stopping because, were that to happen, such an event could connect all sorts of thoughts, even unthinkable ones. Almost everyone in our family, and in other families close to our home as well, connected their lives, the precise completion of their activities, to the constancy and precision of our clock. They no longer even trusted the clock on the tower of the city post office, visible from all sides. It had once stopped and refused to go. Our clock was the most faithful in the city.

Travel

When my mother was young, she completed the only two trips that she took in her lifetime: one to Greece, the other to Italy. Although these travels were a long time ago, she relived them constantly. She embellished them and reworked them in her memory so that, in the end, these travels had changed so much that they bore very little resemblance to the actual trips themselves.

When fate held her down in a new city in the Balkans with her family of many children, when life lost its normal order, and restlessness and uncertainty set in, my mother would relive her old travels ever more intensely.

The more difficult her life became, the more she altered her long-ago travels. She sought a happy diversion. She wanted her current life transported into her former travels to find there some escape.

Her life flowed in these circles of illusions.

She never lost the impressions made by her travels in Italy. At times the cities she had once visited, Rome, Bari, Brindisi, and Venice, represented planets in the happy galaxy found within the depths of her consciousness and in the domains of her dreams.

She passed on her Italian travels to us children. The Italian cities she visited were a reality that lived and expanded within us. We continually traveled there, expanding and embellishing her journey in our minds. Everything she had seen, everything she had touched and tasted in Italy, gave meaning and blossomed within her. From the few Italian words she had learned she began to create short but clear sentences. Out of the few Italian sayings she had accurately memorized she created new constructions; she organized her knowledge. She was helped a great deal in her study of Italian by the old peacock-shaped radio that my father had brought from Constantinople during his solo trip abroad. From the nearby Italian radio stations we listened to, Mother picked up several great arias from Italian operas sung by famous artists, and she hummed along. Later on, everyone in the family sang them. During times of hunger or war, when we were in bad humor, one of us children would start to sing an Italian aria, and soon the whole family would be singing, as if we had been transformed into a small chorus singing to my mother as a sign of our love. We carried these refrains from the days of our happy childhood into our adult lives; they echoed ceaselessly within us, bringing with them our mother's image from the time of the happy embrace of our childhood with her . . .

The Bomb

During the years of wars and migrations my parents maintained a sort of strategy of silence in front of us children in order to save the family. We never understood why, before we were to move again, our father would suddenly disappear, only to reappear either just before or just after some dangerous event occurred. We never, ever understood this crisscrossing through wars, dangers, and death during both the wars and the postwar years.

"The Italians came again to Pogradec," my mother would say, beginning the old story with new words but never-changing content.

Even though we knew the details by heart, we children wanted to hear my mother's voice, the pleasant, ringing voice of our destiny.

"Yes, the Italians arrived," continued my mother. "And they stayed a short time, those wretched men. Those men were not cut out for war . . ."

We knew what came next. We waited for our mother's words: "Then the Greeks came, and war flared up between them. We were a big family, and we were quickly divided in two. Some parts of the family were under the Greeks, others under the Italians. There were days when the sun rose on Italian rule and set on Greek. And, dear children, sometimes it went the other way around. It was hard to understand what was going on. War, war is such a cursed thing . . ."

When she reminisced about the war, my mother would fall silent. Silence overcame her. She, poor thing, had seen what war was. During the years she was left without my father, when she worried about events in the Balkans because of the news she heard and found ever more difficult to understood, she would often ask us, "Children, what are they saying? Is there going to be war?"

"No, Mama, there won't be war."

"It is you children I worry about. My time has passed. Please don't let there be war. Please don't let there be war . . ."

"Please don't let there be war. Please don't let there be war . . ." This refrain was always with us. When war broke out in Vietnam and innocent people were bombed, I remember once, after hearing on the radio that if the monsoons came, the bombing would stop, my mother said instinctively, "May God grant that the rains come . . ."

Now she brought us back to the time of our childhood, to the time during the war when she saved the family: "Children, where did I leave off?"

"When the Greeks and Italians were fighting in Pogradec!"

"Ah, yes, poor me. If things had gone just a little bit differently, I would have lost you all. None of us would be here."

A bomb, a bomb had fallen on the house!

"How did we survive?"

"I will tell you the whole story in order. Before he left, your father had ordered me to keep everyone in the house, to go down to the cellar and wait there for the bombing to stop. Here in our house by the lake, right next to the market, we had everything we needed, enough food and water to last a long time. . . . That was all well and good, but, wretch that I am, something deep inside gnawed at me, telling me not to stay here. We should flee from the basement with food and water."

We children listened to my mother's story—who knows how many times she had told it before—with unaffected wonder. Then she calmly continued.

"No, I said, we cannot stay here! I gathered up all of you children, I took two bags of food, and we set off for my mother-in-law's; she lived with one of our unmarried aunts in territory controlled by the Greeks. During the night there were bombs dropping from every direction. It was hellish . . ."

Even though we knew the ending, we always listened to Mother's words with fresh amazement: "After two days had gone by at my mother-in-law's without a bomb striking, I returned home into Italian territory to get the rest of our food. Bullets whizzed over my head. Who could tell, for heaven's sake, whether they were Greek or Italian? They were bullets like all other bullets, black and nameless . . .

"I went down into the basement where we were supposed to have stayed during the bombing. What should I, poor thing, see there but a bomb, a bomb that had fallen into the basement.

"Oh, poor me, this would have been our grave!"

She composed herself and said, "Oh, my dear mother, you made me lucky the day I was born so I could save my own children. Once I had calmed myself, I looked around the basement. I cannot describe the hell I saw there. I had a large earthenware jug filled with oil. It had shattered into tiny shards. The oil was spattered all over the walls. In my travels with your aunt in Italy I had bought a large set of dishes, white porcelain with blue stars. The entire set was smashed to pieces. The little stars were all gone.

"And here, my dear children, we passed death by."

Flags

*D*uring wartime we stayed alone with my mother in our small house by the lake. During our childhood there was more war than peace. Peace came to us only through my mother's great calm soul. Yes, even during wartime her soul radiated peace, security, and hope.

Whenever Father sensed danger for the family from a nearby war, he disappeared in secret and prepared for our future resettlement.

At such times, Mother took on Father's role in the family as well. There were several events that we would not have survived without her. There was nothing that those times did not bring to our town, located at the very crosscurrents of history. Every important event that would take place in history first took place in our town. Troops went to war through our town.

My mother usually got a flag from the soldiers or she sewed one herself. We children did not understand why our mother collected flags from the various armies when they occupied the town or abandoned it. Since the time of the Turkish wars, all kinds of armies came here for a short time or a long one.

When the Italian soldiers came to Pogradec my mother bartered bread, oil, flour, and other foodstuffs for an Italian flag, and when the Greek troops came she bought a Greek flag from them.

Everyone wondered why my mother bought these flags, but when the Italian soldiers came again, she displayed their flag from the roof of the house. As a result, the Italian soldiers did not lay a finger on our house. However, it drew the attention of an Italian unit whose soldiers stopped in front of our house wanting to set up a machine gun on the roof because it jutted out more than any other in the city.

My mother had found herself in this position before, when Italian soldiers occupied Pogradec for the first time. Then she saved us, thanks to her knowledge of Italian. It had not been easy. We children were in tears, and we pushed our way into the argument. The Italian soldiers' hearts quickly melted. They forgot all about the mortal danger. One soldier thought I looked like his child. He took me in his arms and cried out, "My son, my child!" He began to sob. My mother brought them quince preserves and rakija.

But now another unit was at the door of the house. Times were different now. On this occasion, my mother did not even have time to display the flag. It would truly have been the end of all of us had my mother's maternal instinct for rescuing her family not done its work again.

The Italian soldiers were retreating in a panic with rifles, bombs, and machine guns. Our house was once again indispensable for the soldiers. They categorically insisted on setting up a machine gun on the roof. We children were crying and getting in their way. They jostled us and pushed on past. My mother barred the stairs. In beautiful but panic-stricken Italian she said to them, "Soldiers, halt! Your officers are lodged here . . ."

The soldiers stopped. They knew that all the soldiers were retreating. But they were caught up short by my mother's peremptory tone in clear Italian, and, unable to recover immediately, they paused a moment; they had never retreated in such circumstances. The lead soldier looked at my mother with suspicion and said in a threatening tone, "Madam, we will come again. If we do not find our men here, things will go badly for you. We will shoot all of you."

Mother had once again chased death from the family. Fate kept the Italian soldiers from returning. Instead, Greek soldiers came. Mother had enough time to hang the Greek flag . . .

The Mother Tongue

Silence is our mother tongue.

Beckett

*W*hat was my mother's mother tongue? Shortly after her birth she became motherless. Her father brought her a new mother. And so, my mother did not, as they say, imbibe her mother tongue at her mother's breast. Her father was a prefect during the first decade of the last century at the southernmost border between Albania and Greece. There were problems in this border zone, as many as you could wish for. Life experience had taught her father to speak Albanian, Greek, Turkish, a little French and Italian . . .

The town of Janina was not far away. There were many of her father's own people there, and, naturally, they had learned Greek. My mother, having been left motherless, was under the care of her large extended family. When she was a bit older, she went to Salonika to live with her uncle who was working as a surgeon. There she solidified her knowledge of Greek. Her uncle was married to an Italian, a real signora, as my mother would say when she let her mind drift back to memories of her childhood, as she often did. She could not forget the woman's large white hat, bigger than any my mother had ever seen. From her, my mother learned a little bit of Italian.

In Salonika during the twenties, my mother saw just how many languages were spoken, how many different lives were lived. At the end of her sojourn in Salonika she could make a list of the languages she had learned and those she came to love. Aside from Greek and Italian, she had picked up a bit of French from somewhere or other, probably from the teacher who came to teach her aunt's children. Had my mother stayed longer in Salonika she would certainly have learned Castilian as well from the Sephardic Jews living there who had professional ties with her uncle. My mother remembered the great white caps of the Sephardim and the language they spoke, which was closest to her Italian yet something else altogether.

My mother never returned to Salonika after her childhood. She remained in Leskovik, but the Greek language had taken root in her forever. When fate brought us to Skopje, a city cut in two by the Vardar, a river flowing toward Salonika and on to the nearby sea, memories of Salonika woke once again in my mother's memory. She spoke often about the promenades by the sea. In her memories, Beaz Kule, the White Tower, continually rose up before her. She recalled the white gulls circling the tower. Now, half a century later, transported to the banks of this river, where fate had irrevocably settled us, she watched several white gulls that had seemingly flown out of her memories. But they were real gulls, Father assured her, explaining how they flew up here from as far away as the seashore of Salonika, bringing the breath of the sea with them. As my mother stared across the flowing river, forgetting even my father's presence, she returned once more to Leskovik . . .

There she was in the bloom of youth. Salonika and Janina were left in her thoughts alone; she would never return there. Those cities were forever connected with her memories of her childhood and of her adopted Greek language. That language, as much of it as she had mastered, held fast in her consciousness. Italian too held its place in Mother's mind; her knowledge of it revived and deepened when she and Father traveled to Italy for the first time. They went from Bari and Brindisi up to Venice.

My mother did not remain unmarried long in Leskovik. Matchmakers came from the distant town across the lake to seek her hand for my father. Her father thought for just a short while when they requested the hand of his only daughter. My mother passed quickly into her new family, into the house by the lake. From her mother-in-law, whose mother tongue was Turkish, she naturally began to learn this language as well. But it was an archaic form of Turkish spoken in the Macedonian city of Prilep toward the end of the nineteenth century.

When in the forties of the past century the Greek-Italian war flared up and spread to our town by the lake, fate caused my mother to revive both her Greek and her Italian as never before. When the Greek troops occupied the town, Mother would communicate with the soldiers in that language so they would leave our family in peace. When the Italian troops occupied the town, prepared to punish the Greeks' supporters, Mother would address them in fluent Italian. The troops continued on their way, and we continued on with our lives.

Soon we crossed the border for the first time, traveling across the lake in the family rowboat, becoming immigrants in a new country. In this new country we had to unravel a new linguistic enigma. As always, our family stayed true to its Albanian language. At times, because of our other languages, those we knew before and those we now acquired— those held in memory or half forgotten—our vocabulary in our mother tongue grew smaller; in this smaller vocabulary we stacked up ever more meanings than our language could support. We compacted into this remnant of language the meaning of our fatherland. Such was our linguistic fate; our exile continued.

In this new country our Albanian language had minority status. My father, my mother, all of us now had to study the majority languages of the country in which we lived: Macedonian, Serbo-Croatian, and Slovenian, which were all official languages of the Yugoslav Federation. We found ourselves in a real linguistic labyrinth. We were often told that if we knew two languages, we would learn a third and fourth more easily. Maybe that was true for the younger members of the family, but not for my mother and father, who were more advanced in years.

In his new job as a Socialist judge and later as a court translator from Turkish, Albanian, and French, my father needed a good command of Macedonian, but he never fully mastered it. My father, who had penetrated deeply into an older Turkish, the language of the Ottomans, discovering the keys to its enigmas, also had a good command of modern literary Turkish after his studies in Constantinople, but he did not have the strength to grasp Macedonian fully. We, his older and younger children, knew Macedonian well—it was, incidentally, the language in which our schooling took place, in a part of the city where it was not possible for us to study in Albanian, our mother tongue—so we usually typed and edited his translations from other languages. Together with one of my older brothers, my father even translated an entire book that was never published; it was forgotten somewhere by someone, though it was eventually published under some other translator's name.

My mother, with just a little schooling in Janina and Salonika, more self-taught than my father, learned new languages with much greater ease. In fact, although she did not have a rich vocabulary, what she knew in each of her languages was clear, pure, and sound.

As for us children, when we went off to school and reached the point of discovering and learning foreign languages, we picked French first of all. My mother, with the little French she had not forgotten, had just what we needed to begin our study; she gave us the courage to persevere on the long road of language study . . .

And after many years, after my mother was left alone, alone with Father's books, we often asked her what language was her mother tongue, since, after all, it was our mother tongue as well . . .

The Holy Books

When my mother was left in her crystalline solitude, with all her children scattered through the meanderings of their lives, she felt a strong inclination toward a piety that had been suppressed for many years but was now preparing to surface.

If Mother believed in something holy, something that brought her closer to God, she believed in her God-given mission: to protect her off-spring, to hold them in her embrace until their wings were strong, and then to let them fly off into the unknown expanses of their lives.

There could be no stronger religion than this. Now that she was left alone with her children and grandchildren, with an awakening godly presence, my mother entered into conversation with God through Father's holy books. She believed that in these books would be found Father's yet-undeciphered messages through which she sensed his living presence.

"Even if there is another life, my dear children, I am staying with you," she often told us as she greeted us while she sat near Father's books. She wanted to read and interpret these holy books Father had left behind in order to impart something significant to us, her children, before leaving us forever, setting off on her path of exile. My mother did not leave her family to burn down like a solitary candle. During the time of life that remained to her she wished to sacrifice herself for us in some new, exalted, and holy way; this was to be her last sacrifice.

There were days when she read the Koran without interruption, pausing at those passages where, beside the hand-drawn and colored Persian miniatures, there was the trace of spilled ash, the trace of the time when my father had read them, cigarette in hand over the opened page.

There were days when she immersed herself in the Bible. There, too, she encountered traces of ash from Father's cigarette, from a time when he had been engrossed in reading. There were also days when she found these same traces of ash in the Talmud. In fact, it was among the pages of these holy books that traces of ash were most often found. Maybe that is why Mother spent most of her time with them, with Father's presence. Her thoughts crossed from one holy book to another, as if across an invisible bridge that was solid in her consciousness and must have been in her subconscious as well. Moving between the two religions, Christianity and Islam, left to my parents in a chain of conversions, my father and mother, in the link of their generation, had acquired a strong sense of the relativity of even the most contradictory truths in life.

Among my father's books my mother also discovered a very old Bible in which, on the back page, in handwriting now almost entirely faded, dates had been inscribed. These were most likely the years in which people were born, dates of the festive and sorrowful events in the family's life. She thought a long time about these inscriptions, for here once again she discovered the traces of ash, remains of Father's frequent return to these pages. Did this writing correspond to the final phases of the passage to a new religion, the transfer to a new holy book, or did this family chronicle correspond to God's presence by way of this holy book? . . .

In an old copy of the Koran, with its Arabic script that Father was so adept at interpreting, my mother discovered handwritten notes next to the numerous Persian miniatures.

Mother also discovered several Arabic words written in Father's hand. She wanted to touch the secret of those words inscribed in my father's mixed script, to compare it with the other handwriting, probably of his unknown ancestors, whose presence was implied by this holy book.

There were moments when Mother regretted that she had not entered earlier into the great secrets of Father's library while he was still living, to interpret them for us, to comfort us in our uncertain exile.

For us as well, many secrets of Father's library had vanished or remained locked in the books themselves.

Dreams of a Lost Time

*F*or everyone in the family sleep was the greatest treasure.

The dreams of poor people know no borders; they are similar the world over. The dreams of poor refugee families are a great treasure. Father and Mother often told us that events in our dreams sometimes took place in the abandoned house next to the lake, on the opposite shore, across the border in our native country. If we had each told our dreams, someone could have compiled a harmonious mosaic of our abandoned country, whose memory had become so faded in the reality of fleeting time and forgetfulness.

Mother's dreams traveled farther, pushing through the labyrinth of the family's abandoned houses. They made their way down to her native Leskovik, to the Albanian–Greek border and beyond; they reached her close kin in Janina and from there went onward to Salonika. She went to her family, to the relatives of her mother, who had died so young, seeking a little familial warmth. In her dreams she found the lost fullness of life. My father's dreams were also filled with ancestors and close kin who came to discuss hereditary land or to give their views on the interpretation of ambiguous deeds of title. My father dreamed of his own land and his own house, to which he never returned and which, through various divisions and confiscations, remained whole only in his dreams.

Our dreams, children's dreams, made their way to the lake, up to the former border, and there they stopped. The dreams reached the monastery at the very border above the lake, the border that divided the two quarreling countries, closed to each other.

Many years later, after the borders had lost their former significance and our dreams had worn away, our close relatives, whom we had not seen for a whole lifetime, came to see us from beyond the border.

Years and years had gone by without our having become acquainted, and yet, the older folks, unknown to us younger family members, told us we were close kin. So we began to tell our dreams, dreams dreamed on both sides of the border, that Balkan Wall. Our dreams were so similar that we could complete each other's, dreams of lost Balkan time . . .

The Power of Languages

During her youthful travels to Italy, my mother developed a love for that country and a particular affinity for the Italian language. For my mother, a language was a country, and she nurtured many countries in her soul.

Late at night, after she had put us children to bed and when my father no longer wished to listen to his distant radio stations, my mother spent much of the night moving the little arrow in the small window of the radio shaped like a peacock with its feathers fanned out, seeking one of the Italian radio stations that could be heard so clearly at night. She then continued her Italian travels for a long time. She stayed up late at night, sometimes even till dawn, dreamy from the music, as if even in sleep her once-upon-a-time travels to Italy continued.

Fascism in Italy took my mother by surprise. Never, not even in a dream, did she expect that her new encounter with Italy would take place in wartime.

The Greek–Italian war flared up quickly.

Our house by the lake jutted out, making it suitable for lookouts in all directions. In the battles that raged in the streets between the Italians and the Greeks, both sides wanted to occupy the house to have a better view and gain an advantage in the battles to come. We children, clustered around our mother, waited for our end to come at any moment.

Death could come knocking at our door at any moment. Our little town could change hands in the course of a single day.

Fear had bound everyone inside their homes. Rumors spread quickly that the Italian soldiers were advancing. The Greeks had not been able to take our house, but now the Italian troops were near. From all around one could hear their cries—*Avanti!* Forward! At last, we heard the sound of rifle butts striking the door of our house.

My mother went quickly down the steps, all of us children in tow. For the first time we saw these curiously dressed soldiers, their large hats adorned with feathers. Instead of fear, we younger children just barely held back our laughter.

My mother bravely opened the door. She addressed the soldiers in clear, concise Italian. Perhaps for the first time encountering their own language spoken clearly by a person deep within foreign territory, the soldiers were evidently taken by surprise, and they lowered their rifles. We children were also surprised at hearing for the first time how our mother spoke Italian. We could not even recognize her. We were filled with pride; fear left us as hope of salvation settled in.

My mother begged the soldiers to leave our home in peace. A soldier with two epaulets on his uniform spoke courteously to my mother and requested that she allow them to set a machine gun on the roof to strike the Greeks if they returned. My mother gathered up the children around her and, as if issuing orders, told the soldiers in her clear Italian to leave our house if they too had a God and children.

Mother, drawing on some hidden strength, which we hardly knew existed till then, commanded these Italian soldiers. She spoke fluently and clearly, with no hint of fatigue. The Italian soldiers were not entirely sure whether my mother was an Italian married to a local or whether this was some sort of Balkan linguistic marvel. In her speech she possessed a kind of inner magic power to command people. It seemed as if my mother had gathered and solidified that Italian language from her first great Italian adventure, which she now heard only on the radio and which, in the actual moment of fate, released its life-saving force.

A miracle had indeed occurred. The commander of the soldiers bowed to my mother, and the soldiers left our house. The Greeks pressed from all sides.

My mother could breathe easily at last. Thanks to her knowledge of Italian, she had snatched us from death one more time. Again and again we children had impressed upon us the miraculous saving power of languages.

Rakija and Meze

At sunset, my father would set down his book on the balcony after a long afternoon of reading; this was the sign for my mother to come with a small glass of homemade rakija.

My mother intuited when my father was in the mood for just a sip of rakija and when he wanted to eat some meze with his brandy. The latter was most often the case when guests arrived, a frequent occurrence.

Mother was a real master at taking little bits of things and turning them into wonderful meze. During the years of poverty and Socialist collectivization, my mother secretly planted some peppers, eggplants, tomatoes, garlic, onion, parsley, and cucumbers in a little plot of land in our garden. She managed to hide them so well among the roses, the carnations, and the obligatory basil that almost no one knew of mother's secret garden. And though they shared the earth with the flowers, these vegetables grew successfully for my mother year in and year out. As the first eggplants ripened, my father would say in jest that the earth itself loved my mother. At that time there was scarcely any such produce in the markets, and what there was quickly vanished, almost certain to end up on tables in great dining halls, which were not open to everyone.

My mother made the best meze for my father and his friends when the vegetables in her garden were ripe. She made an unusual salad from finely chopped parsley and used the leftovers for her yogurt dip, made from buttermilk that had, in turn, been made from the milk of our hidden goats. When my father's friends came over, I started hanging around just for the meze. My father and his friends did not notice how quickly the appetizers disappeared. From time to time my father shot a stern glance in my direction, but to no avail. Later on, when I was a bit older and was included in the conversations between my father and his friends and allowed a sip or two of brandy, I ate more, way more, than I drank. The food still disappeared quite quickly. But my father no longer scolded me. With time it became ever clearer to me that between the rakija and the meze, the time and the conversation, there was some sort of order, some mutual consent not easy to achieve . . .

The Taste of the Dough

During our years of increasing poverty, my mother's skill at shaping dough into surprising shapes was all that remained alive of her love of things Italian.

In her travels to Italy she had made a lasting discovery: how to use the magic of shaping the dough to free us from the sad reality of our poverty and hunger. She was perhaps the first who, before the Italian occupation, brought to her native land the secrets of spaghetti, macaroni, lasagna, and many, many other Italian enchantments made of dough. With a little flour and water, and much love and artistry, she indulged the dappled illusions of our childhood.

Although, in actuality, we always ate the same dough throughout our days of poverty, it always seemed as if Mother had made us something new.

She of course followed the family traditions of mixing dough to make Balkan-style noodles, round loaves, pitas, bureks, and rolls, but with the added Italian magic for shaping the dough, she increased our sense of her Mediterranean dream, the illusion of her travel from long ago. No matter how much my mother wished to retain her memories of that distant Italian voyage, the passing of time brought forgetfulness; and yet she never forgot how to shape the dough Italian style. That had become a part of her life; it was in her blood. It had become one of the bare necessities of our life.

My mother passed on to us children her love of twisting the dough into ever more fanciful shapes. Often, our mouths filled with the doughy shapes, we felt the touch of our mother's hands. This taste lingered a long time in our lives, even after we had left behind our years of poverty.

Holiday Tikush

*I*t was only on festive occasions that my mother made tikush. We children looked forward to holidays most of all because of Mother's tikush. Tikush is a kind of Balkan pie—of unclear origin, like much else in the Balkans—made of flour, milk, eggs, and chicken (or possibly lamb, if available). First you mix the flour, then you roll the dough in two pieces. You set one of the rolled layers of dough in the pan and cover it with pieces of meat and a meat broth mixed with a custard made from beaten eggs and milk. You then place the other thinly rolled crust on top. It all gets baked in an oven, though, of course, the tastiest tikush is baked in a baker's oven or set on cast iron over hot coals.

My mother learned to make tikush from my paternal grandmother, and she in turn from my great-grandmother, and so on back through the ages. My mother passed on the secret of tikush to my sister and to her daughters-in-law. We began to eat tikush more often, not just at holidays but at other family meals as well. Yet, the taste was different somehow: it could not come close to the taste of my mother's tikush during the time of our poverty and the Socialist ration books.

Stalin's Portrait

My father slaved over his books until late in the night. He waited for all of us to fall asleep so he could continue to read and to think, having found new energy from the strength released by our dreams, as he used to joke. My mother did not go to bed before my father did; she always found something else to do.

On one such late night in the spring of 1948, a mob of people we did not know burst unexpectedly into our house. First, without knocking, they came in through the balcony and into the room where we children were sleeping.

My father always said that the most securely closed doors are open doors. As a result, our house was always open.

My oldest brother woke up first; he jumped down several stairs and immediately ran to my father to tell him that people had broken in and were looking for the family's portrait of Stalin. Usually, above our heads on the wall of our room hung two large, beautifully framed portraits, one of Stalin and the other of Tito.

My father never showed uncertainty or fear in front of us children, even when fate struck its hardest blows against our door. It immediately became clear to him that the time of "Big Brother" Stalin was gone forever! For a long time he had heard the Western radio broadcasts he listened to in secret after we went to sleep, in particular the BBC, reporting that something serious had happened between Tito and Stalin, but he had not believed them.

Now my father calmly waited to be led away by the people who had entered the house looking for Stalin's portrait.

There were very few reasons in this life to believe in Stalin, but it was obvious why we kept his picture next to Tito's. It was simply for the safety of our family, the safety of us children.

My father calmly waited for the people to lead him away on account of that portrait.

Before, it was those families without portraits of Stalin who were under suspicion. But now . . .

There was not much time to think. He got himself ready to go. But instead of the police at the door, there was my mother standing in the doorway to his study, carrying in her hands the large framed portrait of Stalin.

The poor thing. Even in her dreams she could not imagine that in her hands she held my father's doom, the doom of our family.

My father, grasping immediately that he had once again cheated death, calmly asked my mother what she was doing with the portrait, since the people from the police station were on their way out of the door of the house.

My mother, not sensing what had just happened, calmly replied, "A few days ago I noticed that there was a lot of dust on the picture of Comrade Stalin. I heard from the neighbors that people from the government were going to come around to see how people were caring for their portraits of Tito and Stalin! So I said to myself, Let me just wipe this picture off. I had it in the kitchen, and I was on my way to show those people, but they're leaving."

My father's blood nearly froze.

"My dear wife, you poor thing, Stalin is over! He and Tito have quarreled. If those people had found Stalin in our house, they would most likely have taken me away. And who knows whether I would ever have returned."

Now my mother was in shock.

She let go of the large picture.

The glass in the frame broke into a thousand shards, each one seemingly refracting our family's fate.

My mother composed herself and said quietly, "Oh my dear blessed God, what I would have done! What a fool! Oh my God! I was running with the picture to our death! Oh my God, what a wretched thing I am!"

"You saved us all," father said to her calmly as he hugged her.

Once again, in our family's struggle to stay alive, life and death had intersected.

Shock Workers

$\mathcal{M}$y father and Mr. K. were busy translating an old text (which, according to Mr. K., was very significant for shedding light on the history of the Balkans) when their attention was disturbed by the voice of a young man from the regional party committee. His voice carried through the window into the ground-floor room where the two old men were working.

"Come on, you old parasites, come out and do voluntary labor. Put your useless papers down. Come join the working class . . ."

My father slowly lifted his glasses; he was so involved in the text that he had not understood what the boy had said while he was racing past.

As soon as Mr. K. observed that the young man was sufficiently out of earshot, he said aloud to my father, "Those ill-mannered louts. They're calling us to the shock worker brigade. We're supposed to go dig up the earth, but we're digging deep into history."

Now Father understood what was going on, and he quietly replied, "If we all do the digging, who will do all the other work?"

Outside reverberated the mobilization song, "America and England will rise up and become proletarian lands!"

Old Mr. K. began to laugh when he heard these lyrics. My father, fearful that Mr. K. would go out and start an argument, continued to read aloud from their translation of the document . . .

"Well, that's their work after all and not ours. Let them struggle for a 'proletarian America and England,'" said Mr. K. consolingly, and, together with my father, he delved into the old text once more.

The Silver Mirror

My mother was left motherless early in her life. From the mother she never saw she inherited a silver mirror. When she married my father, there, amidst the items in her dowry, shone the old silver mirror. This mirror accompanied us in all our migrations.

Mother never parted with it. Often, late at night, she would light a candle and illuminate the silver mirror. Long into the night she would whisper to it.

Father knew that Mother confided in the mirror, but he never enquired what she asked it.

While we children were growing up, we interpreted Mother's devotion to the silver mirror in different ways.

Most often, Mother summoned her mother in the mirror, as if they were engaged in a silent dialogue.

My mother said farewell to all her closest kin when we made our great migration across the border. Only several steps beyond that cursed Balkan borderline, and her life changed forever; she was cut off from her family, from the brothers who stayed behind, from all her closest kin.

For nearly half a century she received brief telegrams informing her of each death. Perhaps by having so many children of her own she wanted to establish some sort of equilibrium. She consulted the silver mirror about everything. Extreme care was taken so that the sacred mirror would not get broken. From way back in her family history, perhaps ever since the moment the mirror was first discovered, it was thought that bad luck would come if the mirror were ever broken.

In the mirror my mother summoned her lost time.

The Medal

*F*or a long time, there, shining among the books, was Father's silver Order of Socialist Labor, third class, the only medal he received during his long working life. For a long time my father had had a secret wish to receive some sort of decoration or medal; he privately wished for this especially after our great migration in a critical year for our family's survival. As a non-party member, his chances of receiving the desired medal were about zero. On holidays our family noted everywhere in the neighborhood many people younger than our father, party members, who sported numerous decorations and medals on their chests. Those who had a larger number of medals wore only the insignia, and those who had only one wore the decoration itself or the large medal. We children could not understand why my father, who worked day and night, did not receive anything, no order, not even a ribbon—while others who worked less than he did had abundant medals.

In our family we always stifled questions whose answers could be sensed but that hovered in the air. Questions were not asked that would only cause more pain.

In poor families, silence is golden. Due to our poverty, silence was priceless.

Our conception of medals was influenced by the Russian movies we watched as children just after the war. Even though we didn't remember the war, we were born just as it began, and now, as we began to comprehend life during a time of peace, the war seemed to begin again for us through Russian movies. We watched only Russian, always Russian movies. In those movies all we watched was the war, nothing but the war. The cries of the war were engraved forever in our young souls; they reverberated far and wide throughout our lives. Engraved forever in my mind is the image of victorious generals with their many ribbons and medals displayed on their chests. Had there been more space on their chests, they would have had even more ribbons and medals. Later on came the era of badges and of shock worker medals . . .

Even then, while we were watching Russian movies with their decorated soldiers and officers, it became clear to us that receiving such an honor was a significant event in one's life; however, whenever we saw who was wearing their medals on national holidays, it was clear that medals were handed out unfairly. This feeling of the importance of being awarded a decoration was strengthened by our father's case: he wanted so much to receive an order of any rank; he needed that or some other kind of medal. We had only an inkling of our father's reasons. It was very important at that time for him to have an order of any class.

At last, one May Day holiday, my father received his Order of Socialist Labor, third class. For us children, this was the most important honor in the world. My father was very happy with it. He was happy with this award only on account of our happiness. He felt that by receiving the Order of Socialist Labor, the last shadow of disloyalty, which could, in those times, hold back the families of newcomers, might finally disappear.

All of us took a turn wearing the medal on our chests, no doubt feeling that we were adding to my father's pleasure.

On May Day my father walked about the city displaying both the order and the ribbon on his chest, even though it was customary to wear the ribbon alone on such occasions. He made several turns around our neighborhood and around the square so that the greatest possible number of neighbors and acquaintances would take notice of the medal.

For a long time after my father's death, my mother continued to polish my father's medal; she then placed it back among the books as if she were looking at my father's happy face the day he brought it home.

Holiday

Reading had a special place in my father's life. He considered it a happy event, a holiday. When he read a true book in the manner he believed was the only way possible, a quiet, festive mood, one we easily recognized, settled on the house.

Then the holiday of Father's library was carried through the whole house, out into Mother's garden, to the road in front of us. In fact, other holidays did not exist for my father; religious ones went by without his notice. Our mother, however, would dress us younger children in our old clothes or those of our older brothers, now clean and neatly ironed, so it would look as if we had new ones.

For several years after he received his Order of Socialist Labor, third class, our father wore it to the May Day ceremony in the square. Later on, it was as if he had forgotten all about it. He considered it sufficient that those who needed to know, knew he possessed it.

So, for my father there was no holiday other than the holidays of his happy reading, of his discovery of a life that he could not in reality touch. Reading was a powerful escape from his exile.

Whenever he read a true book, selected in the order he had assigned to his books, an order whose significance was known only to him, he would put on the old, worn-out tie that went with the suit he could no longer wear that he had bought as a young man in Constantinople years before, because this was his holiday.

For a long time my father remained faithful to his personal holidays rather than to public ones. By keeping his holidays of deep, concentrated reading, he maintained in his life a certain balance whose significance he alone knew.

Ration Books

Families with many children, families of working miners, and families of those with other strenuous jobs had the right to receive extra ration books each month. With these Socialist coupons one could buy a strictly rationed amount of sugar, salt, oil, soap, and other staples. At first glance it was justice, an exemplary division of poverty.

My mother received the ration books from my father at the beginning of each month, and she kept them in a hidden place so that they would not get lost somewhere and leave us to go a whole month hungry, unwashed, and without salt and sugar.

During the long period when these coupons were used, we were left without them on only three occasions: the first time, one of our goats ate them; the second time, they had fallen behind the wall cabinet, and my mother found them only after they were no longer valid.

The third and last time we lost the coupons was mainly my father's fault. He remembered sticking the whole month's supply of coupons into one of his many books while he was engrossed in his reading, but he did not remember which one. Mother, who was well acquainted with just about all of Father's books, spent days sadly leafing through them in search of the ration books and watching as hunger increasingly gnawed away at us, her children. Even her magic trick—of making every imaginable kind of pita with the remaining bits of flour and watered-down oil from the month before—could not quiet our hunger for long. We paged through Father's books, our stomachs grumbling; we read a bit here and there, looked at unusual pictures, thinking we might read these books someday, but we just could not find the Socialist coupons.

Weaker and hungrier than ever before in our lives, we waited for the end of the month, for our father to bring home new coupons. Then one day, our father's friend Mr. K. came to return one of the books he had borrowed. As soon as my father opened it, out fell the ration books we had been looking for—the coupons, no longer valid, were useless. We looked sadly at Mr. K. He looked at us in amazement.

My father often wanted to learn from Mr. K. his impressions from reading the book he had borrowed. Mr. K. was the same way with books he lent my father. This was how they maintained their durable friendship. When a book was returned, there frequently ensued a short argument, even a heated discussion, usually provoked by the fact that the book had not been read in its entirety or because one of them had falsely stated that it had been. It was not unusual for Mr. K. to voice his opinion about a book even if he had not read it. From time to time, my father grew suspicious of the improvisational nature of Mr. K.'s pronouncements, but he never had conclusive proof. Now, however, he waited.

"Did you read through the whole book?" my father asked Mr. K. coldly.

"Of course!" answered Mr. K. categorically.

My father picked up the coupons that had fallen from the book and said to him, "If you had read the book, you would surely have brought us these ration coupons, which are now good for nothing."

We children, ravenous and weak, looked with scorn at Mr. K., who had been responsible for our hunger.

Mr. K. immediately grasped what had happened. He looked at us children, his innocent victims, with sadness and compassion. A few tears rolled down his cheek.

We children retreated, but our feelings toward the sin of the unread book stayed with us.

A Coin
in the Trevi Fountain

When in Rome during the thirties, during the one and only trip my mother and father ever made together, my mother threw a coin into the Trevi Fountain.

Roman legend says that a traveler who throws a coin into the fountain will surely return to the Eternal City.

Years passed, decades, a half century of life in the Balkans, my parents lived from war to war, occupation to occupation, with no chance of reaching a time of peace.

My mother never forgot about the coin she had thrown into the fountain. She hoped, in vain, but hoped nonetheless, that one day the Roman legend would come true.

Every spring, in the garden of our old Turkish house where the aromatic carnations and roses blossomed, where the first lilac blooms carried the breath of springtime, my mother revived the little fountain that splashed the blossoms in the garden.

Just as my father cleaned his library and put things back in order, freeing the books from their accumulated dust, so too my mother tended her garden. The library and the garden . . .

My mother often recalled the Trevi Fountain when, kneeling beside the fountain that was the source of her garden's beauty, she told us about her long-ago trip to Rome. We could never understand why it was always here that she would tell us about the Trevi Fountain as she knelt beside her little fountain in this blossoming patch of earth in the Balkans.

My mother told how the maidens and the prancing horses had turned to stone in the very heart of Rome. The play of sunlight on splashing water seemed to bring the maidens and white horses to life.

With their last strength, Agrippa's brave warriors, defeated in mortal battle, at the gates of death, and parched for reviving droplets of water, approached a beautiful Roman maiden, who revealed to them a spring, the first fountain—the fountain of salvation, the Trevi.

My mother dreamily spoke about the legend, about her once-upon-a-time encounter with that Roman beauty.

For years, the waters of the Trevi Fountain splashed in my mother's Balkan dreams. But fate did not intend for the legend to come true for her...

After many years our country opened up; now one could travel easily to Rome, and we told our mother that the time had come for the legend to be realized. She, however, did not want to destroy the dream of her long-ago travels. But she was happy that the legend would come true through her children's imminent travels to Rome. For her, this was the legend's fulfillment.

La Rinascente

*I*n my parents' fifty years of married life in the Balkans, years through which world wars and Balkan wars were interwoven, the only trip they took together was to Italy in the thirties.

In Rome's large department store, La Rinascente, my father bought my mother a beautiful blue dress with white polka dots, a dress she wore for many years and then kept for still more years, for decades, for half a century.

As they were leaving the department store, my mother was presented with the large annual catalogue of La Rinascente's original fashions for that one year out of the decade of the thirties.

This was the first time in her life she had seen such a brightly colored book, with its numerous photographs of different outfits and household items. Though she had seen many other books in Father's library, this was the first time that a book had been given to her, one quite different from all the other books she had known until then.

My mother kept this book beside her two holy books. She often paged through it, finding amazing clothes with ever-new splashes of color, dresses for every season of the year, children's clothes, jewelry, household furniture. In her father's house she had seen a few pieces of such furniture, but never in the little town deep in the Balkans where life had set her down in search of family happiness.

When my mother first returned with my father, gladdened by her once-in-a-lifetime trip, she misplaced the Rinascente catalogue somewhere, but, fortunately, she soon found it and returned it to its place beside the holy books.

Many years passed. The fashions in the catalogue became outmoded. But not even those outdated fashions could reach us here. Following the pictures in the catalogue, my mother sewed, tailored, and combined pieces of fabric, but many things were lacking to make clothes like the ones on the models.

In those rare moments in her life when she had free time, my mother paged through the Rinascente catalogue. The pages transported her back to Italy, to the time of the fashions depicted there.

When the family's migrations to who knew where began, my mother never parted with her catalogue. Its pictures stood in sharp contrast to everything that was and was not available in the Balkans. But in the catalogue my mother had everything she wanted.

Then came our greatest exodus from the little town nestled by the lake. We would long forevermore for the banks of the blue waters where we had first set down our roots.

Eventually we found ourselves in the large city beside the river that led to the sea. This was our family's final relocation. In the course of time there were temptations to move farther: once you have abandoned your native hearth, the source, why not travel onward to the river basin, onward to the great ocean? There were all kinds of opinions, false hopes, prudent delays, but, for whatever reason, the life of the family continued to flow beside this big river.

"We will set down roots here," my father had said, and, indeed, we stayed there forever.

My mother, poor thing, lost her Rinascente catalogue during this final move. Most of Father's many books survived the move intact, but Mother had not wanted the catalogue to get mixed in with his books, and so it was destined to be lost. Maybe it was a good thing that my mother lost the catalogue, because the postwar years brought with them an even greater contrast between the poverty of our time and the pictures of clothing and other items displayed there. There was also a danger, during the Stalinist era, that someone outside the family would see the catalogue and denounce us for keeping foreign propaganda. This worry was always in our minds because there were similar incidents, arising from even more trivial causes, during those years.

And so it was that my mother lost her catalogue, but the words "La Rinascente" remained in the family's vocabulary with their old meaning unchanged. The image of the lost fashions of the 1930s stayed alive within us.

For us children, La Rinascente was a living book, one that had befriended us for a long time in our childhood. From the start, La Rinascente had supplemented our first primers; the fashions of capitalism from one of those forgotten years of the 1930s contrasted with the pictures of the construction of Socialism in our school textbooks on social studies, geography, history, and Marxism.

Mother had shown us, through this catalogue, that there existed another world beyond the sea, another life that she had once seen and experienced, and that one day this life here would merge with that other life there, and there would be only one life. We nodded our heads as if everything were clear to us, and we waited in vain, we waited for such a long time, for our mother's promise to be fulfilled. That was how my mother explained things while she had the catalogue; after it got lost, we remembered its bright, shiny, colorful pictures, which my mother now made more vivid in our memory—that is how deeply imprinted they were in hers.

The family's final move took us further away, much further away, in fact, from that other life of which my mother had spoken and that we had seen in her catalogue. After the war came hunger. Before we had had at least something, now we had nothing, but we had come through the war alive, which was most important, so anything could happen . . .

When the difficult consequences of the war had eased a bit and we had become accustomed to our poverty, our family slowly set down roots in its new environs, secure in the trust that came through our coexistence with the residents of the city surrounding us. We easily befriended many of them because they too had the troubles that newcomers have.

When Father began to organize his books again, it was a sign that the city, like the family, had passed through its moments of uncertain existence. Mother once again began to dream about the Rinascente catalogue. As a matter of fact, one morning she said aloud that she had dreamed of her lost catalogue. She assured us that it was here in the house, even though we all knew she had lost it in the move. She recalled the Rinascente pictures even more clearly than before, and she wanted once again to revive within her memory those days of our family's life together. She wanted to re-create them out of the flour that we received with our first Socialist rations and from the black market—the latter an activity at which my brothers were extremely adept, easily trading for flour the things from the United Nations relief packages, especially the canned, sweet-tasting meat that we never got accustomed to eating. Using the flour and remembered recipes from her Rinascente catalogue, my mother supplemented the Balkan symphony of dishes by rolling dough into the never-before-seen shapes of macaroni, spaghetti, lasagna, and ravioli with a sauce made from the tomatoes she herself tended in the garden, where she also grew roses, carnations, and ample amounts of basil.

In my parents' life together "no" was never an answer. Frequently, instead of "no" there would be a tentative, protracted "yes." But definitely never "no."

We children were witnesses to this. We always felt deep within us the illusion in search of happiness, which matured into peacefulness, which then flowed for a long time in the family. One had to catch the sound of this calm and pass it on to other families. Really, one had to.

After hearing our mother's dream, we searched the house for the catalogue for a long, long time, even though we knew it was not there. Our mother's dream had to be taken seriously. But the catalogue was not there, and that was that. We then hatched a secret plan to write a letter to La Rinascente, asking them to send a new catalogue to our mother. We would tell them about the old catalogue in our letter. We wrote the letter in an international language. At the dawn of the 1950s, to compose and send such a letter to Italy was an act of both bravery and folly, but it was also a great fantasy that the letter would reach Italy and, if it did, that the catalogue would make its way back into our mother's hands . . .

Stalinism was over and done with; the country was free. The borders were opened, except for the most condemned, which we still had in the Balkans. Yes, people were free, free to travel, free to be happy, but the fear, the fear remained.

One evening around this time, when my father was deeply engaged in his reading, my mother told him that she wanted to send a letter to La Rinascente to request that they send her the newest catalogue. Father could not give an unequivocal "no" as an answer, not wishing to violate the family's sacrosanct rule in conversation with my mother.

At first, my father nodded his head doubtfully, as if mainly to himself. He wanted to say something that was of significance: the Stalin era was surely not quite over; Stalin was always here; he could easily return to inflict his cruelty on Tito and on everyone else! My father wanted to pass on the latest news he had heard while listening in secret to the British radio station, the BBC, but he did not say a word.

A letter to the West at that time would have constituted lunacy. Absolute lunacy. Naïveté. Who would write such a letter at such a time to the West? And, on top of that, just for an ordinary, an absolutely ordinary catalogue! A letter like that would be absolute proof of spreading foreign propaganda, of spreading capitalism.

Until then we had communicated with foreign countries only by telegram. We communicated only by telegram with our relatives still living in the country from which we had come because the borders were eternally closed. And, when we did correspond, it was only to pass on the news that someone had died. My mother had many such telegrams, a whole necropolis of them.

And now that custom was to be broken to communicate with Italy, a country that was until recently Fascist. For a simple, ordinary catalogue one was to risk the family's peace and its future. That was too high a price, even an impossible one, my father thought.

My father did not say a word of this aloud, but my mother well understood his silence, which was at times clearer than words themselves. And that was where the conversation ended . . .

Now fear, real fear, gripped our tender souls. We were overcome by a great, uncontrollable sadness that we skillfully hid from our mother.

The era of de-Stalinization flowed turbulently onward.

We wanted this new wind of freedom, the opening of the country, to blow strong enough to carry our letter to Italy and to bring back the catalogue from La Rinascente. We woke in the morning and went to bed at night with thoughts of the catalogue.

Big things were happening in the Balkans. But, for us children, the biggest event took place one morning when the voice of the postman cut off our sleep: "Package from Italy."

My mother thought she was still in her old Italian dreams and acted as if she had not heard a thing.

Now the postman cried out more loudly: "Where are you people! You have a package from Italy!"

We children got up at once.

We knew very well that this was no dream. We accepted the package calmly, and my oldest brother signed in the designated place in the postman's booklet. We were gripped with immeasurable happiness, but also hidden fear. It took only a second for us to open the package and free the catalogue from its several protective layers of paper. At last, the luxurious pages of the new catalogue from Rome's department store, La Rinascente, were before our eyes, showing the spring fashions for 1950 . . .

My mother slowly came toward us. Her eyes glistened with happiness.

"La Rinascente! La Rinascente!" she cried out happily.

"You're right! La Rinascente!" we confirmed in unison.

So much joy and happiness at the same time almost completely pushed away our fears. We had brought my mother's dream to life, the dream of her forgotten Italian springtime.

My father appeared out of nowhere. He joined in our happiness. Looking at the new Rinascente catalogue for the spring of 1950, my father said, mainly to himself, "They are coming, surely better days are coming."

The Balkan Wall

The borders in the Balkans were a lethal sign not only of divided countries, divided rivers, lakes, snow on the mountains, but also of the divided souls of the people.

The borders ached . . .

The borders stopped the flow of time for many people, for families, for generations. The borders enslaved and devoured people's time.

Because of those accursed lines in the Balkans we were always in exile. We carried the borders in our very core. Every war—and wars were frequent in the Balkans—brought with it new borders along who knew which route, severing the land, the families, and life itself.

"Borders, borders, curse them all!" was a common refrain in our family.

When my mother first crossed one of the Balkans' many borders fifty years earlier, she could never have dreamed, could never have believed, that so much time would pass before she would return to her native country to see the members of her family who remained there and those born since she left. There were others, older than she was, who did not live to see that day.

The Stalinist regime of my native country, which lasted the longest of all other such regimes and was the most contemptible in the Balkans, finally considered my mother sufficiently old to be no longer a potential threat to important state interests. During those years, the border was opened only for older people, those with white hair, those whose peers on both sides of the border were nearly all dead, those already tottering up to the brink of death.

My father spent a long time considering whether my mother should undertake such a trip at this point in her life. He knew very well that a trip there would cause her greater pain than coming home again. But there was no force that could stop my mother from making this trip she needed to make in order to complete her life. My mother had long ago crossed the border in her mind; now she crossed the other border . . .

The years of half a century had taken their toll. She could not get hold of herself, she could not get accustomed to her native land. She silently cursed herself over and over that she had ever undertaken this trip. Father's words about the curse of return rang true. She said to herself that it would have been better, infinitely better, if she had gone to her grave with her old dreams to continue her illusions there; perhaps that would have let her see her native country and her kin more clearly. But, what happened, happened.

She had to spend two months in her native country, not one day more or less. That is what was written in red ink on her visa. Her close relatives and immediate family who remained there showed her the greatest possible attention. As she later told her daughters-in-law when she returned, they held her in their arms, they washed her feet in a basin of water and dried them.

It was only with great difficulty that my mother became accustomed to the goodness, the closeness, and the beauty that surrounded her. She went from family to family. People arrived, relatives from both sides. Some she recognized, others she did not. She was soon overcome with tiredness and worries.

My mother, brave and strong in life, forthright among different nationalities when rescuing her family, accustomed to various faiths and nations, now, here, in her native country, felt, as though for the first time in her life, closed in, powerless, and defeated. With the last of her strength she struggled deeply, both consciously and subconsciously. She wanted to be strong and happy this time as well. After all, why wasn't she happy? Both fortune and misfortune had come to her life as parts of her destiny. She accepted them without thinking much about their true essence. But she could not act in a way contrary to herself, contrary to the deep internal core of her being. She struggled with all her might to hide her feelings, to be different from what she was. But never in her life had she pretended to be something else, nor could she be now. Her close relatives sensed what was happening, but they could not understand. My mother finally decided, with relief, to seek permission to leave several days before the date stipulated on her visa. Her relatives were worried. This would be the first time ever that someone left before the visa expired. If she had requested to stay beyond the expiry date, that would have been understandable; they would have found some solution. But, in this case, everyone was worried. My mother was insistent. There was no way around it.

And so my mother found herself at the border again.

She found herself first at an enormous two-winged gateway covered with hammered nails, chains, numerous padlocks, and, right in the middle, a gigantic lock, constructed as if intended to lock up time. Yes, exactly, to lock up time itself. Her time. Her family's time. The time that had been stolen from her. The time that had been stolen from all of us. Our time.

She looked with fear at that gigantic gate. She saw it as a great wall, the greatest wall in the world. It was the great Balkan Wall. The wall of divisions, a cursed wall, a wall she kept tearing down in her thoughts.

Her close relations, worried, held her hands. They understood her pain, their shared pain. Be that as it may, they had to obey, to submit to a funeral march led by fear—the fear emanating from this cursed Balkan Wall, from this cursed barbed wire, from all the borders crisscrossing the world of people. None of my mother's close relatives asked any longer why she was leaving. They were silent.

My mother entered the small border guardhouse. Before handing over her passport, she looked for one last time at the terrifying face of Stalin in the picture above the guard's desk. In the instant she glimpsed his face it seemed as if every moment in the life of our family rose up within her. She recalled Stalin's portrait that hung in our house at the end of the 1940s, when our whole family could have been destroyed, when we were saved by luck alone; she remembered the many families who suffered because of Stalin. For her, the Stalinist era was deeply buried, but here in front of this high Balkan Wall life had been breathed into him once again. She could not compose herself.

My mother walked alone toward the great gate. A young soldier in a light olive-drab uniform walked in front of her. He unlocked the great gate, which screeched as he turned the large key, a key as large as the revolver at his belt. Then, with visible effort, he pushed the great gate open, shouldered his machine gun, and addressed my mother: "So, auntie, what was so bad about being in your own country that now you're leaving early?"

My mother looked at him thoughtfully and with great pity, the way she looked at us children when we did something wrong and did not want to own up to it, but she did not answer him right away. The time it took her to answer his question seemed to last an eternity. It was clear to her now that she had been right to insist on an early departure from this country. In an instant she turned over in her memory the course of events that had occurred in just under two months. For this slice of time she had to pay some price in order to return. There was nothing that they did not ask her; there was nothing they did not stir up in her deep and expansive soul. But she, poor thing, withstood everything; she accepted it all as ordinary, normal, natural. No one could pull her away from her natural, quiet strength.

Most likely the border guard had directed this last question at her automatically, as a form of rebuke. But, she remained as she had been her whole life: direct, forthright, frank. After all, there had been so many obstacles in her life, armies and soldiers had approached her at the door of our house with machine guns and bombs, and she had come out the victor. The soldiers had respected the depth of her spirit, which protected her children. There was some kind of solidarity in the depth of people that connected them, bound them, and she came out victorious. The family always continued on with their lives, always approaching the next curve of fate.

Now here before her stood this young soldier, a poor kid—how many soldiers had she seen? A bit abruptly, but in a natural tone of voice, she said to him, "Son, you ask me and reproach me for leaving this country ahead of schedule. My country is where my children are."

At that moment the soldier did not have a ready answer; he had no prepared comeback. The gate creaked again as the strong wind pushed it open a bit farther. My mother set off. But before she crossed the border, she heard the soldier's last words, surely his own words this time: "What nationality are you, auntie?"

"I am the nationality of those I live with, son."

My mother crossed that Balkan border once again, but the soldier remained with his solitude to interpret my mother's answer.

Prayer

*I*n her later years, when the quiet sunset drew near her, after she had set her children on their way, after she had welcomed her daughters-in-law and delighted in her grandchildren and great-grandchildren, after my father died, my mother began to feel deep within her that the time had come to return completely and eternally to God. Not that she had distanced herself from God in years past. God could not be far from her life; that was her fate, though she experienced it more subconsciously than consciously. After all, hadn't she always said that God himself had given her life only so that she could save her children? In her lifetime she had given birth to many children, but she had lost many as well. Cursed life. She struggled with divine strength to conquer the life that was fated for her.

And so, Mother's secret but lasting piety returned, reawakened, not as a debt to be repaid to her earlier faith but as holy submission to her loneliness in all its mysterious forms. She returned, finally, to her prayers. She prayed regularly and with devotion. Earlier, when she was at the peak of her physical strength and the whole house weighed on her shoulders, the family routine itself seemed to be her daily, constant prayer. But now she was discovering a new dimension to her prayers with which she held back her great loneliness and the silence. She intensely believed that through prayer she was closer to her people, those who vanished on the other side of the border, whom she never saw.

In her moments of transcendent prayer my mother seemed to travel out of her body, across the border; now she was with her kin, her closest family brought back to life. In fervent prayer, in secret whispers that overtook the quiet, my mother told her people her unspoken words, words held in and shaped over more than half a century.

At times, prayer filled my mother as a gentle infusion of silence itself, a profound encounter with all dimensions of her existence. Her closest family, vanished long ago, visited her in her great, dreamlike prayer, where at times she was more present than in life itself.

My mother remained devotedly faithful—she could not have been more so—to her great prayer as she sat by Father's lonely books. This was her sacred time, the lost Balkan time, which she alone could bring back through prayer. Through prayer she quietly evoked all those she loved. As soon as they left her quietude, passing through the warmth of her heart, her words were endowed with some sort of holiness.

Then, more than at any time before, my mother was close, closest, to God. Her body was transformed into spirit, crystalline, her prayer—her connection with God.

At that time my mother believed in the holiness of her prayer life and in its power to connect her to all the dimensions of time and the exits from it. Her prayer restored to her all her time unlived with her closest family—the dead, the living, and those out of reach.

In her prayer my mother often whispered lines from Father's books, still open from the very day of his passing. My mother's prayer, in a manner understandable to her alone, revived Father's presence through his living books.

She knew well, and often assured us children, that all prayers reach one God, whatever his name might be. At the sunset of her life, Mother managed to draw enormous energy from all her prayers through her great and continued sacrifice.

My mother had only one unique God in all her prayers. In those moments of prayer to which she surrendered herself more fervently than ever before at the sunset of her life, we secretly watched her beside our father's opened books—whose significance remained indiscernible to the end—and we felt her soul expand through the blissful expression on her face, through her strong love for us, through the price of her suffering and sacrifice, and through her strength and then emerge lightly from within her, from its own borders, out into the expanses of her prayer.

Tears

*N*ever in our lives did we see our father cry, really cry. Nor did our mother cry, or at least we never saw it. How many torments had they experienced, how much had they suffered in their lives, with us, in their wanderings in the wilderness, in the labyrinth of our exile. In their eyes we never saw tears of torment, tears of relief, tears of happiness.

The tears were always contained somehow, held back by some kind of dam that they could not cross. And life always held new challenges.

We never, absolutely never, saw real tears in our father's or our mother's eyes. Only Father would sometimes, privately, shed tears while reading the fate of his family in one of his open books.

Many years later, after his passing, I was leafing through his old books, through the pages in which he had been most engrossed and on which, deeply absorbed, he had let fall ashes from his cigarette. I would see the ashes, stuck fast by Father's tears, like wondrous miniatures, holding my father's former presence, the meanderings of his secret thoughts as well as my mother's constant presence and her wish to settle on some part of the earth where she could build a strong nest in which to settle her many children.

It was possible now to trace Father's tears, pressed forever in his books.

After my father was gone, when my mother remained the final guardian of his books and of their order, she often sought the pages that held my father's tears and the ashes from his cigarette.

On one occasion, when we found her in a strange frame of mind among Father's books, she revealed to us, as if coming out of the orbit of her constant silence, a secret of her life with Father and with his books.

Once when my mother was bringing him tea, she had come upon my father, absorbed in a page, tears in his eyes, talking, sobbing. At first she was frightened. What could have happened? Had some news come from the other side of the border telling of yet another disappearance, the loss of close ones, news of painful events?

It was then that he told her the secret: he was writing and discovering pages of his family's unknown fate; he was bringing back the memories of his ancestors. But the price of coming to this most powerful idea was to wet it with the dew of his tears. He could not touch this decisive truth without passing through the purification of tears.

My mother calmed herself with difficulty.

Mother held inside all the tears that Father cried in those moments. The opposite also happened, more rarely. My father kept his silence about everything my mother told him. We children barely sensed the quiet sobbing that came from Father's books, at times held back by his pensiveness.

Yet, we never saw our father in tears. He remained forever with a cheerful face, with gentle vitality in his expression, and with a secret readiness for good . . .

Part Two

The Margins
of My Father's Books:
The Constantinople Dream,
in Search of Lost Time

*M*y father's spirit lingered most of all in his books. In his emigrant fate the books stifled and covered over that second personality that, in those who are uprooted, is by nature always pronounced. My father succeeded in passing on to us children, to all his children, his great attachment to books.

My father's library was the great escape in our lives. All life was contained in the pages of my father's books. If life was for him a passage through hell and purgatory, then his books represented heaven. He collected books from all parts of the world but mainly from the countries of the East and the Balkans—as many, according to his calculations, as he would be able to read in his lifetime. These calculations proved incorrect: many books remained unread; there were books left for us to read in order to discover our father's lifetime, his lost time, the time that was dedicated to uncovering the Ottoman era in the Balkans.

There were two strong currents in my father's soul, two turbulent rivers that flowed continuously but never touched, never merged, never terminated in the distant sea of his thoughts.

One current represented his instinct for preserving his identity, for raising it on a pedestal at the borderline between the ordinary and the extraordinary; the other current represented his readiness to contextualize the question of his identity. In search of his definitive opinion, he gathered experiences from the Ottoman temporal magma, from past times in the Balkans. How many nations, powerful or weak, autochthonous or later arrivals, disappeared, assimilated into one another? How many faiths were interwoven in the people's souls? In his life neither stream dominated the other; their waters never merged. Borne within each was an unresolved riddle from that Balkan part of hell from which there was no clear exit.

My father's life passed, flowing across several countries and faiths, across quests through manuscripts in diverse languages.

To the end of his life he remained unbound to any one fatherland, one language, one faith, or one ideology.

At the final moment, sensing, almost instinctively, the danger, he pulled away from possible exceptions and settled in no fatherland. To the end of his life he remained faithful only to the country of books and to their ideas.

Among his books there were always grammars and dictionaries of the languages he needed to study and master, languages of those nations whose fate, it seemed to him, was interwoven with that of his own nation. He had a similar attitude toward the holy books.

There among his books were old handwritten versions of the Koran, an old edition of the Bible, a copy of the Talmud.

It was possible to find among his books valuable works about the Janissaries.

For a long, long time I could not understand why he collected books about goats. But later, in the course of time, this too became clear to me. In Father's books one could discover his strategy for the survival of his family in the Balkans, one of the most troubled spots on the planet.

The Third Exit

There, in the scorched heart of Constantinople, there where Atatürk would wage his final battle for Turkey after the abrogation of the sultan's rule and then the caliphate, there in the flaming battle for the survival of all the subject citizens—all the peoples that had just recently belonged to the empire—while the Turks sought to salvage what they could of their core essence from the ruins of their empire, my father was overcome, as never before, by a deep existential disquiet. At the end of the empire, Constantinople ended in flames.

The marble dream of the palace that had been inhabited by twenty-five sultans was coming to an end in irrevocable agony. Thousands of minarets burned like firebrands; in the macabre dance of their shadows they illuminated the palace for the last time in this great imperial city. The magnificent caravanserai, the celebrated madrassas, and many monumental edifices went up in flames. All that could be saved was saved. The pigeons circling the great mosques once again discovered their peace.

My father walked pensively among the wounds left by defeat. Atatürk was rescuing the Turkish soul; he was saving Constantinople. But *my father*, what could he save? Whose soul *should* be saved in the new Constantinople? If he accepted the victories of others, of Atatürk, this would surely be a defeat in his life, the sweet defeat of his own life. It would be yet another circle of hell in his own inner betrayal of his family and of himself.

He could never quite determine how far he should go against his own people to make things go well for him, or to at least have the illusion of going well. He contemplated the ashes of the life-and-death struggle of yesterday's empire and of others; he could not accept this struggle as his own because he knew in advance that he would always be defeated.

His return to the Balkans became his ultimate decision. He thought that if he returned, he would escape that cursed line of Janissaries through which the young people of his nation had passed for centuries and which always retained its youthfulness thanks to new victims. He did not want to be sacrificed before the gates of heaven; he would perhaps have been happy to be sacrificed before the gates of hell. For him, there was no third exit.

The True Path

When my father was considering the various relocations of his family, his thoughts would quickly reach the intersection of two paths. One led eastward, toward Constantinople and Cairo, the other toward the West, to Rome and Paris, and, from there, to America. For him there was no third path. This was the crossroads at which many of the family's predecessors had found themselves.

Unlike his predecessors, my father had traveled along both those roads and had returned: first in the twenties, when he spent time in Constantinople and Cairo, and then, toward the end of the thirties, when for the first and last time in his life he traveled with my mother to Italy, visiting Rome, Bari, Brindisi, and Venice. My father held on to the memory of these travels his whole life, never exhausting them. If that memory wore down, he revived it during difficult times in our lives. My father spoke so often about Constantinople, and my mother so often about her trip to Italy, that we children adopted their travels as our own.

My father often pondered the meaning of these two trips within the context of his family's uncertain fate. In his heart he felt that it would have been, at the same time, both easy and difficult to steer the family galley toward the east, toward Constantinople. In traveling to Constantinople he would have continued the family's unbroken procession through time; there we would have had a secure material mooring and refuge. This travel reached its happy conclusion in his thoughts; at times he was unhappy because it had not happened in reality. But those moments were rare . . .

As much as it had fascinated him in his youth—and my mother constantly kept the idea alive—travel to the West through Italy was uncertain and difficult to accomplish. There the link between the family's distant ancestors and future generations had long been lost. In other words, no third solution was possible. He had to remain in the Balkans with his fate.

He remained in the Balkans, condemned at its very roots, with the certainty of wars to come. He followed some sort of family instinct for survival, with all the possibilities for misfortune it carried, into the uncertain and contingent fate of the identity he preserved.

At a Crossroads in the Labyrinth

*W*hen he entered Constantinople for the first time, he was overcome with an intense excitement. This two-thousand-year-old city had the means to captivate his young soul. Intoxicated by its unparalleled splendors, he walked around this enchanting city for days and nights on end; he found ways out from the warren of narrow alleys and emerged happy at the crossroads.

He stopped along the quays of the Golden Horn and quickly developed a kinship with the sea. In the distance he watched the ships returning from or departing to Europe or distant Asia. He had heard a great deal about Constantinople from his mother, but what he saw with his own eyes was more powerful than any words could describe. It was worth pouring one's youth into this wondrous city with its boundless opportunities.

Constantinople became his Paris. Fresh in his mind were the images and ideas expressed in Balzac's works, which he read with enthusiasm. He learned French, just like every other true Balkan autodidact. Balzac was his most beloved author in the world. He also read Stendhal and Flaubert, but it was to the works of Balzac that he most often returned. Often, as he stood at the Golden Horn, he imagined himself as Eugène de Rastignac after old Goriot's burial, when he declared war on Paris from the heights of the Père-Lachaise cemetery with the cry, "Now it's between you and me!"

Many Balkan intellectuals could be found in their own Paris, some different city, uttering the same cry, yet still wishing to celebrate in the true Paris their victory over the Balkans. Later, he would direct a nearly identical cry, but for different reasons, against Constantinople in search of a way out toward his Balkans.

Later, when he discovered Mr. K., his lifelong friend, Mr. K. revealed that he had had this same illusion in Paris. This was yet another reason for them to join in lifelong friendship . . .

What would happen in his Balkans, or in his nation's part of the Balkans (he knew quite well that not a single ethnic group in the Balkans lived on its territory alone; these lines were changed by force of war, and then for decades, for centuries, each nation mourned its cursed fate), what would happen in the Balkans in the next fifty years, in the years of life that remained to him, in the life of his nation, in the life of his family, that had first to reinforce its ties with his father's line?

In the glistening lights of Constantinople, at the height of his youth, he needed to turn toward his Balkans, released after five centuries by this Ottoman realm just at the moment of its collapse. Yes, he was here, in the very place, in the ruins of an empire, to draw lessons about this time and future time. He could not have imagined that he would re-experience the fall of this empire through the fall of two more empires and that his life ultimately would be enclosed in the circle of the Balkan family he had yet to create.

He had not yet started his family, but he feared for his Balkan fate. It was clear from the beginning that he would not remain in this city, where, were he to change his name and accept a new citizenship, he could create a new family. But, because he wanted to influence his family's fate, fate often took cruel revenge on him. Each attempt at imposing his will carried unforeseeable consequences. Everything led him toward the labyrinth of fatalism, but he resisted; he searched for his pathway of resistance in the great human labyrinth that was Constantinople.

Now, at its very source, in the ruins of Constantinople, my father, deep down, even in his subconscious, was profoundly tormented by the thought that one day all the malevolence of the Ottoman Empire, all the machinations of the government, including the curse of the Janissaries, all the curses of calculated divisions, would be revived in the small Balkan nations, in each individually or in all of them together. He deeply feared that a new, smaller Ottoman Empire would impose itself regardless of what or whose emblems it carried. Five centuries was no small amount—generations in the life of a nation. Anything could happen.

Now that the crust had been lifted on the Ottoman magma, stifled lives and nations that had long been suppressed could grow from their immature larval state into monstrous dragons. He feared that one of the newly freed nations of the Ottoman Empire would adopt the recent methods of the enslaver and so become the enslaver of those smaller than itself.

There were moments when these thoughts were so black, so difficult, that he contemplated—though deep within he was certain that this could never happen—lingering in the easy destiny of Constantinople's splendor, to link his fate with the privileges offered to him by choosing Atatürk.

Should my father have obeyed the call of Atatürk's command, directed to the young intellectuals of the Balkans, to save the fatherland?

"People like you are needed": this phrase echoed in him to the end of his life.

What battle should he have waged when defeat was unavoidable?

In his search for a possible exit, he gave himself over to his books and to his studies. In the labyrinth of his books he could find a happy way out, or at least the illusion that such a way existed. He remained mostly in his books. These old, dead manuscripts, whose forgotten interpretations he sought the keys to unlock, saved his life more than once, even during the time of those empires in which he had determined to sacrifice his life and the life of that family he had first to create.

So my father's life flowed through several fatherlands. Rather than choosing one as the definitive one—assuming he could have known which one it was—he resolved to have several and to remain faithful to his books alone, his one true fatherland.

He did not have the sense, nor did he ever develop such a sense, that he was connected for all eternity to one fatherland, one language, or one faith; he later passed on this attitude to us children for us to reconcile in our own lives, each in his own way, some with greater success than others. Some diverged more, others less, from our father's path in life.

His children found themselves at different crossroads in the labyrinth, left to solve in different ways the vicious circle of our own fate starting from the place my father had reached. It remained up to us whether to stop there, to continue from the point of the vicious circle where my father had stopped, or to abandon ourselves to new concentric circles—but our own—of that fate out of which illusions more than reason made us believe a true exit could be found. But there could be no true exit . . .

Between Constantinople Heaven and Balkan Hell

*I*n Constantinople my father escaped several traps to which he could easily have fallen prey had he not from the very beginning made peace with himself and with his decision to return to his family, to whom he would remain most loyal. Returning was a more compelling fate than all others.

He knew that Atatürk's victory and the defeats of Beyazit and Suleiman, the Magnificent, even the defeat of Abdülhamid, were not, and could not be, either his victories or his defeats.

He could not hide the shadow of his own unique life among these victories or defeats. It was time for decisions, time for a definitive choice.

How many more times by the Golden Horn would he bare his heart to the sea, to the waves, and to them alone reveal that he had decided to return? Return was now his final decision. Atatürk's words would never cease to reverberate in his mind, particularly at that moment: "It is necessary to save all that can be saved from the old Ottoman Empire, to save the soul of Turkey. It is only with people like you—young, courageous, from the very heart of the Balkans—that salvation is possible!"

Here in Constantinople, in this mosaic of the Balkans and of the world, he was called to the rescue, he was called upon to save his family in the Balkans; everyone awaited his help. Yet his own life flowed, moved on, and dispersed like these waves on the shore of the Bosporus.

Trapped between the heaven that was Constantinople and the Balkan circle of hell that awaited him, trapped between the lands of his mother and those of his father, he had come once again to make his decision and to confide in the sea. He was trapped between his mother's heaven and the loneliness and hell of his own identity. He knew deep inside that all his conflicting decisions were already resolved and that he was now opening his heart to the sea in vain.

What was left for him to take away from Constantinople except his memories and his dreams, dreams he would spend his entire life trying to realize in his Balkan hell?

He had decided on the hell where his family waited, where the knot of the Ottoman era had not yet been untangled.

Most loyal, the most loyal of all to him, were his books. He, in turn, remained most loyal to them. It was as though, in carrying away the books, he also carried away his Constantinople time, a time preserved only in them, a time he could continue to live, explore, and enrich. He was left in the labyrinth of his books to seek the exits from the Ottoman era, to seek a fortunate escape for everyone in the Balkans.

My father was sure that an Ottoman Babel would still persist; it would thrive in the small, unprotected Balkan kingdoms. They would entangle the paths between East and West awhile longer. They would remain within the labyrinth without escape.

He took his books with him, his great friends, his partners in conversation, his collaborators in life. Life was impossible without his books. His books were his life with all its illusions. With the books, it was as if he walked his living library through the Balkans. In the end, he deeply believed that, until his death, books were his only exit.

Mission

When my father was leaving Constantinople with the books he had collected for the towering Babel of his own Balkan library, he also took with him many books written in the old Arabic script, whose demise was being prepared by Atatürk's reforms.

The prohibition against the old Perso-Arabic script, which had served in the Ottoman Empire and in the initial period of the new Turkey, seemed to provoke a contrary reaction in him.

He imagined himself as one of the last prophets of the old script and set himself a sort of sacred mission: he considered it predetermined that he would fill the gaps in the knowledge of what had occurred during the Ottoman era in his own Balkan nations, events inscribed forever only in these manuscripts, which were sacred to him.

He feared that the fall of the Ottoman Empire on the field of war, something he considered a real possibility, given the lifespan of all empires, would give rise to a tremendous and ill-fated unrest in his Balkan Babel.

Until these nations acquired their own networks of institutions—which they had not had in the Ottoman period, or, if they did have them, they were incomplete, or they had some but not others—they would truly be the damned in Babylon.

He felt that many accounts needed to be settled with the Ottoman era. Therefore, in his decision to return from Constantinople, a decision reached largely due to the instinctive call of his family, he discovered his mission of restoring to his nation that which had been lost together with the vanished Ottoman time.

He attempted to find an excuse for Atatürk, who insisted on destroying completely the old Ottoman imperial ideal, but, for himself personally at least, he did not succeed in finding one. He managed to find his own oasis in the ocean of the Ottoman Turkish, or Perso-Arabic, script, where he could calmly chart his own course toward the ocean of time layered in this script.

He had the illusion that there was an exit. His whole life was consumed in pursuit of this illusion. It is curious that it was the uprooted, the foreigners, the Levantines who remained more faithful to the old Ottoman ideal, or at least to some aspects of it, than the Turks themselves . . .

So what was he now seeking in the Ottoman Empire, in the agony and the inertia of its fall, when Atatürk, its very savior, had clearly and categorically declared a return to Turkish roots, to Anatolia? Other dreams tormented my father at the crossroads of these Balkan labyrinths, where there hid, perhaps, another identity, enigmatic and problematic, that was difficult to discover in the swiftly changing vision of the politician or in the vision of both the victor and the fallen.

It remained for my father to interpret the truth in his books written in Ottoman Turkish. In them he was stronger; with them he possessed all time.

The Game of Defeat
and Victory

$\mathcal{M}$y father would often walk deep in thought from the Dolmabahçe Palace and, without realizing it, would arrive at the Karaköy Bridge. Here he was captivated by one of the most wondrous romantic vistas in Constantinople, with its fantastic towering Dolmabahçe Mosque, whose silhouette was mirrored in the blue waters of the Bosporus, creating for him the illusion of departure. Here he often contemplated the significance of the triumph and the defeat of empires.

The Ottoman Empire's existence was maintained throughout the changing of illusions into the disillusion of numerous generations during the course of a full five centuries. The illusions were similar yet different for all the peoples who lived in the great Ottoman magma.

What did the end of an empire mean? My father could see and feel it at close range, he could touch the defeat, and he could sense his part in the repercussions of that defeat. The final Ottoman strongholds fell in the Balkans, in Asia, and in Africa. The Muslim Brothers, on whom most people depended and from whom lifesaving support was expected, were the first betrayal. The fall of the Ottoman kingdom could have been a victory for the Turks themselves, an escape for them alone. However, the defeat was total. A mere seven years was sufficient to put an end to an empire that had been built over nearly seven centuries of countless victories as well as defeats and the subjugation of many peoples . . .

In this game of victory and defeat, in the despair and the illusions of the peoples under Ottoman rule and of the Turks themselves, my father could, with difficulty, discover the direction of his fate. He knew that life had instructed him well in this, that true bravery was not to lose one's sense of reality.

He well knew that, for him and for his nation, for the peoples of the Balkans, there was neither defeat nor victory, merely survival. Yes, it echoed deep within him, bravery is to see events flow past such as they are, not as you wish them to be. This innate feeling about bravery almost never betrayed him, and it was almost always what saved his life, both his life and the life of his family. He was well aware of this. Later on, he struggled to impart this feeling to his children, to all his heirs. He succeeded in varying degrees. Different times bring different customs.

Janissary Fate

What could he take away from the spiritual remains of this destroyed Ottoman time, of this damned Babylon with its jumbled alleyways, with its emptied labyrinths—harems, marketplaces, cemeteries, mountains, a Babel of lost illusions for many generations. Like other Balkan intellectuals, he did not mourn the fall of the empire, but he did mourn the false dream, the lasting illusion, that had given meaning to his life. He regretted that some people in the Balkans would not immediately understand and come to terms with the fall of the Ottoman Empire, especially the fall of the caliphate.

He worried that the fear the Ottoman Empire had instilled would remain in the souls of the people for many years. Historically, whenever an empire fell—he had learned this well from history—fear burst and dissipated. He knew that many tribes on the summits, on the hills and towering mountains of the cursed Balkans, would remain loyal to the sultan and to the caliphate, even when they no longer existed.

He wanted to return to settle these people's accounts with that era. Perhaps he wanted to be a small, unseen Atatürk of the Balkans. He wanted to have an anti-Janissary fate. He believed that the Balkans would be truly saved only when the people freed themselves from their Janissary destiny . . .

What was left for him to take as the last moments of the Ottoman era flowed away?

He could take a genuine step, a step away from this time.

He could win this battle with time, but only if he accepted its reverse current.

The current of his illusions.

The curse of the vicious circle of identity.

He could easily win this battle with time, but he knew that for him there could be neither defeat nor victory, merely survival, if in the era of Atatürk he kept within himself the spirit of his people's Janissary tradition.

Many accepted this tradition; they became renowned in Atatürk's state. They changed their names, their fatherlands, their families, their surnames, and they became a part of the new Turkish realm.

He knew very well who these Janissaries were. There was no greater misery in the world than the Janissary tradition, a curse that awoke every hundred years. He was very afraid that he would awaken the Janissary within. Surely it had existed in his family line. There was, in fact, no family in the Balkans that had not been touched by the Janissary curse. Even after the institution of the Janissaries had ended, many remained Janissaries in their own lives. My father had closely examined the local character, the *Homo balcanicus*, the man for all seasons; he observed that the Janissary institution was simply a facet of the government, of the despotic, absolute power of the sultan.

Many remained Janissaries throughout their lives without even realizing it. Somehow, the Janissary instinct had become rooted within them.

Their descendants struggled to root out these Janissary traits, but they were unsuccessful. When it came to rebellion, revolution, or war, the Janissary seed germinated without anyone having planted it there, in the people's souls.

For years, my father collected all sorts of books, testimonies, deeds, reports, proclamations relating to the Janissaries so he could understand, as far as possible, the essence of this institution that had been a part of the great mechanism of Ottoman power. However, he arrived at the truth that fear and fear alone was the reason for the appearance of the Janissary tradition. Fear built up in people—after rebellions, the collection of tribute, changing faiths. The battle for survival led through labyrinths of fear. My father concluded that when people are freed en masse from fear, outbursts of suppressed opposition break out with greater pent-up strength.

Did Atatürk really free the empire, Turkey, from its accumulated fears? Hadn't they triumphed over the "Ottoman realm" and, therefore, triumphed over their own fear?

Father was afraid that the Janissaries would live on forever in the Balkans. He feared that the curse of the Janissaries would remain. He feared that the Janissary seed that had once been sown in the souls of the peoples of the Balkans would germinate once again.

From his books Father knew perfectly well that the Janissaries, under different names but with similar goals, had existed in other empires. They were already present in the ancient Chinese kingdom, in the Roman Empire, in the Austro-Hungarian Empire, and even in the newer empires, especially Stalin's. Indeed, wasn't Stalin himself a Janissary? The Janissary corps attracts Janissaries. There you have the cursed vicious circle. My father said that one could even compile an encyclopedia of Janissaries in which the section devoted to the Balkans would most likely be the longest. It was surely like that and could not be otherwise . . .

The Key of Destiny

*W*hat was to be my father's final legacy from the Ottoman Empire before his departure from Constantinople? The collapse of the Ottoman Empire was taking place not only in Constantinople during that time he saw unfolding before his eyes. He was certain that the Ottoman era would remain unsettled in the Balkans for many, many years. There remained many unresolved questions that Atatürk was solving under his sword.

My father, for example, was obsessed with the question of faith. What had happened to faith, to the sharia law that he had studied in Constantinople? Now, just as he finished studying it, Atatürk had renounced it! It is true that, had my father wanted to, he could easily have adapted to the reformed law code, established according to European, especially Swiss, models. But it was difficult, difficult to resolve the question of faith and the rapid reforms that Atatürk conceived and implemented, his policy of secularization in particular.

My father knew that, in the Balkans, among the Islamic population in undeveloped rural areas, this would be much more difficult, if not impossible, no matter how much time passed and how hard the winds of European democracy blew. There were peoples in the Balkans who had since pagan times and through the course of the five-hundred-year Ottoman reign maintained the continuity of one single faith. But his nation was perhaps the only one that had held onto three faiths—Muslim, Orthodox, and Catholic.

Once again, the fate of the Janissary was offered to him, now at the time of the ultimate collapse of the empire that owed both its splendor and its collapse to the splendor and collapse of the Janissaries. Why should he consciously choose to be a loser again? My father knew a great deal about the independent, anti-Janissary fate of the Albanian hero Skanderbeg, and he wanted to act in accordance with that part of his destiny. Skanderbeg's resistance echoed down through the centuries toward an indifferent Europe.

My father was conscious of the fact that, ultimately, chance is the determining factor in history; it sets events in motion, and then, later, people find themselves subjugated for centuries. It has always been this way: chance condemns the life of the family, the nation, civilizations, and empires.

As much as he believed in the absolute and decisive role of chance, my father did not permit himself to fall into the philosophy of fatalism, which flowed so strongly through his consciousness during his years in Constantinople. In fact, throughout his life he developed a strategy for confronting fatalism. Perhaps here too lay the secret of his decision to leave Constantinople at the peak of his youth, when his prospects in the new Turkey were bright and his prospects in the Balkans cloudy.

My father was aware that, throughout history, since the time of Skanderbeg, his nation had always been part of a Janissary network, including the intellectual Janissaries such as Sami Bey Frashëri, who had been developing into the father of the new Turkish culture, with his encyclopedias, dictionaries, translations of the European classics, works from the field of the new Turkish linguistics, and literary works, yet who did not forget his own Albanian nation, arguing that he had two souls in one body. In essence, according to my father's reasoning, the Janissaries had two souls in one: the one always held the other down without ever completely suppressing it . . .

My father knew very well that no matter where he went, in Asia Minor or the Balkans, the Janissary fate would always follow him and that his victory would be as pale as his defeat. My father was aware of the fact that if he consciously made the error and did not acknowledge the sin of the Janissaries, it would pursue him forever, but if he acknowledged it, if he accepted a new path, he would have a chance to be saved and to continue his uncertain path through life.

In fact, Father considered himself to be fated to be a Janissary. He considered that the Balkan intellectual, wherever he is found, must, through self-discovery and self-awareness, purge himself of the Janissary in him.

The Balkan intellectual who has not freed himself from his inner Janissary will be primed for national or, better yet, nationalistic extremism, through which he will further confirm his Janissary fate; he may conceal it or suppress it, but it will always be ready to burst out when history turns its course, as it always has, toward chance, toward that final arbiter of time . . .

My father maintained that deep in the soul of each Janissary was a door that remained forever locked and to which someone else always held the key—or perhaps such a key did not even exist. If the key were ever discovered, a very rare occurrence, one almost never witnessed it, and if, after much suffering, the soul were opened, an unseen strength would be released, the volcanic strength of an entire nation would surface, and nothing would be able to stop it in its path to liberation. It would be sufficient for one such person to be freed for the nation to discover its true demiurge. In the course of history, the souls of such people were awakened when the nation demanded it. Now, after the fall of the five-hundred-year Ottoman reign, there had to be more people like this. My father strongly believed in this.

The Waves of Illusions

*H*e came to Constantinople with his old childhood dream of settling accounts with the Ottoman era and to discover the curse at its very roots, to discover when those roots had become entangled, when everyone in the Balkans was left to be pounded by the waves of fate. He found himself in that city surrounded by three seas, between East and West, that city that would forever mark his life, at a true crossroads in the Balkan labyrinths. To the end of his life he felt himself tugged between East and West. The curse of being always caught between East and West, never quite in one or the other, was passed on to his future family as well and, later, to the country where the waves of his uprooted destiny tossed him ashore.

In the vortex of his youthful dreams, impulses, and beliefs he would come here to the seashore by the Bosporus, beside the bridge on the Golden Horn, to confide in the sea, to reveal to it his thoughts, to raise his spirits. But in the dense, deep blue waters at the bottom of the Golden Horn everything was cursed, silent, and still. It was as if the sky itself had turned into the sea and kept silent the secrets it left on the bottom.

Here, deep, deep in the sea, rested his lost Balkan time, the time of his family, of his nation; it was as if, in its depths, he sought conversation with his ancestors. Even the sun could not reach down to the deeper layers of the water, to the layers of retrievable history.

He came to the Golden Horn to a belated confession, to be cleansed by the waves of history, which forever spread and broke on the shore.

He came up to these waves, which always began anew; they encouraged him, they gave him courage at each new beginning of his Balkan fate. There was no other path, nor exit, just new beginnings, new waves. But this suggested confrontations and unrest.

Here, at the Golden Horn, he summed up what he had come to understand during his time in Constantinople, he confided in the sea those decisions from which he never again turned away. Here, in a moment, he anchored his life at its new uncertain beginning.

He could have stayed in Atatürk's new Turkey to continue the modern Janissary tradition; he would not be the first nor the last of the echelons of Janissaries from the Balkan nations that had formerly been embedded in the powerful Ottoman Empire and now in the new state of Atatürk. In the depth of his thoughts, clearer than the dark waters of the Bosporus, it was obvious to him that if he but entered into the trap of a new identity, he would never leave, he would lose himself in the grayness of the new hierarchy. He did not want to become a Janissary, a servant of this new era; he did not want yet one more layer of the turbid Bosporus to cloud his exit out into the quickly flowing waters of his own turbulent identity. He set off along the cursed path toward the Balkans, toward his old family, which was dying out, and the new family he must first discover and then perpetuate. His witnesses, the companions of this new decision, this new path, remained the books he gathered in Constantinople.

The Debt to Time

*H*e often stood before the Golden Horn, as if before an imaginary Balkan altar, to tell his troubles before the many witnesses, before the many citizens of all the Balkan nations who found themselves after the fall of the Ottoman Empire rushing to solve the great dilemma—should they go East or West, toward Europe or Asia, toward the Levant or toward Europe? . . .

He knew that with the end of the Ottoman Empire, a new era was beginning for all the Balkan nations, which had till recently been part of this empire, an era overflowing with unresolved dramas, tragic conflicts, disputed borders, and shared myths. They could not free themselves of Ottoman time; they were its captives.

Later, nearly all the greatest misfortunes of the individual Balkan nations resulted precisely because of this flow of time past, in which their lives had not yet been carried to the end; this time still owed them something; they were its greatest captives. And each generation had to settle its own account with this time, either becoming its new hostage or postponing confrontation for future times.

Yes, he would reflect aloud, all the Balkan peoples have a common past in the Ottoman Empire, with mutual discoveries still to be unearthed, shared myths and legends, with shared pain and lasting grief. They all have their part in the Janissary fate, they are all parts in the mechanism of this government, new for Europe, at the gates of Europe, but a mechanism Europe tolerated nonetheless.

Here, in the swirling currents of Ottoman territory, beside the three seas, between the East and West of his hopes, he was compiling a library in his quest through the Ottoman era.

It was more than certain that his life would unfold, as it had begun, under the sign of these paradoxes.

There was no other way.

He consolidated the key books of his library.

He zealously collected books about languages, about the old Perso-Arabic script, about old competitions between languages, about the Janissaries, about faiths. He knew that these key themes would recur again and again in the new history of the Balkan peoples. While the themes of languages and faith had an obvious future because both were eternal and universal for all humanity, it was difficult to understand why he dedicated such a large space in his library to the Janissaries, to the institution of the Janissaries, to that old, expired, cursed phalanx of soldiers. He feared that the Janissary curse was deeply planted in the souls of the peoples and nations of the Balkans and would be uprooted in future centuries only with difficulty.

The significance of my father's books about the Janissaries remained unclear. Here were the most messages, reflected both in the arrangement of these books in my father's library in relation to the other books, and in the Western and Eastern writers and other sources, which had differing approaches to this horrible human theme in the continuous Babylonian game, always with new means, with sword and blood . . .

Between East and West

*H*ere beside the bridge at the Golden Horn, his coiled destiny unraveled.

He wanted to tug at the string of his fate to understand who he was, where he came from, and where he was going.

There are moments in life when you know who you are but then are condemned to keep on seeking yourself throughout your life, searching along one thread of existence for those moments in time when, in a flash of insight, you know yourself.

He knew better than most what it meant to be born and to live in two worlds, in multiple fatherlands, and not to possess a true one, to feel like a foreigner at home.

To have faith but to be faithless.

He did not know whether the East or the West was his fatherland. There were exits, comforting possibilities along both the Eastern and Western paths. He was often convinced that the East casts its eye where the West fails to take notice.

The East draws together everything that the West draws apart.

And vice versa.

His whole life was stretched between East and West; wherever he went, in whatever country he set down roots, he felt pulled in both directions.

Now, when the Ottoman Empire was at its end at last and he found himself on the heap of the empire's spiritual remains, he was again beset by countless questions, as though he were confronted with the beginning, not the end, of the Ottoman reign.

There were too many questions to unravel for both his generation and those to come.

A person can never free himself from his past; he remains its slave until death.

Fortunate are the nations that have no history (he recalled the words of a certain French historian), yet, as he himself concluded, there is no nation without history.

Of all the problems he wished to solve in connection with the Ottoman era, he was most captivated, most haunted, by the apparatus that had held his people, and all the others, under five hundred years of Ottoman rule.

He did not want to be radical in his views or to end up with the extremists; he wished to arrive calmly at the truth, to his part of the truth. He knew that all honest, brave beginnings lead toward the truth, and there is only one.

He did not want to fall into a constant state of thinking that something Promethean, fateful, and unconquerable had allowed the Balkan peoples to preserve their identities during the five-hundred-year Ottoman Empire nor that it was the tolerance of the enslavers alone that had saved these identities.

Even though he wished to penetrate deep into the labyrinth of the Ottoman era, tracing the lines of eastern Perso-Arabic script, he did not do it on account of some aesthetic pleasure nor to live a life of ease; rather, he was seized by more profound motives and desires.

He wanted solely to bear witness to this time, to return it to the Balkan peoples who had only a vague memory of this era.

He knew that his endeavor, in the conditions that he anticipated finding in the Balkans, would be a grand illusion, a great utopian fantasy, but he could not work, truly function, even live if there were not some grand illusion ahead of him, part of that fated uncertainty that the peoples of the Balkans shared as their common fate. Everything he undertook, and all the books he selected, were steps toward his grand illusion, to discover through the intersecting pathways of his soul, the exit from the Balkan labyrinths.

In his heart, he deeply believed that to offer up his life to this illusion was a small sacrifice.

So this heir to Don Quixote, one who shared his illusions but was raised to follow a different path, believed that there was a way out, and he walked with the melancholy of a Constantinople scholar, his library in tow, among the ruins of the Balkans, which were collapsing further under the onslaught of new Balkan conflicts.

Sea Dream

My father often came to the shore of the sea by the Bosporus as the sun was setting in the distance. He approached this sunset as if he wanted to overtake the sun and return it to the past.

He followed the blue clouds of pigeons' wings that rose above the tall minarets of the mosques. In the distance, the bittersweet strains of a mandolin flowed on as if calling to the opposite shore. There were the white walls of the Dolmabahçe Palace, which shimmered as it commanded the largest share of the Bosporus shore. Here the Ottoman era was most intricately entangled.

He heard the sounds of the last parades, the final sighs of the sultans, pashas, and viziers contemplating their failures.

Visible in these palaces were the styles of every era, of all the peoples of the Balkans, of Europe, and of Asia and those yet farther away, everywhere within reach of the Ottoman Empire's power.

He noted the antique colonnades, the Gothic and Romanesque figures, the many shapes in rococo style, white marble arabesques; there on the facades were dancing bouquets, the marbled interplay of flowers and plants, of sea flora and fauna, wondrous marble medallions so intermixed, so interwoven, one unending image merging into another, this shape so forcefully or gently combined with another that nothing could separate them, and thus they remained forever combined, grotesquely fused.

This former kingdom had, it seemed, wanted to extend this fusion as far as the Balkans, binding the destinies of people, attaching immature and incomplete times to those that were complete and well-formed, intermingling faiths and fates.

He saw the image of the Balkans in the European ambitions of the sultans, the viziers, the high functionaries of the Ottoman Empire.

When the sun had set on the Asiatic shore, he would walk for a long, long time toward the European shore of the Bosporus.

The sea waves washed from one continent to the other. From the distance the boats of tired fishermen mournfully approached. He wanted his steps to hold the line that separated the dry land from the sea, a line condemned to eternal change, digression, and unrest, just as he felt the dividing line within him.

The fishermen caught up with him on the shore. They spread out their white nets on the fine sand, casting onto the shore the deep breath of the sea.

Onto the dry land was cast an entire underwater world destined to make its last gasp, still bearing witness to the depths, the mystery, the antiquity, the eternity of the sea, to the secrets of the dark waters, from where, perhaps, the secret of humanity rose up as well.

He stared at the starfish, which, in their final agony, struggled to straighten their arms and be, for one last time, stars, then dying star-shaped on the shore, remembrances of the mysterious sea. Over there were the blue, treacherous jellyfish, which slowly evaporated on the dry land, multicolored shells carrying messages from drowned galleys and the final sighs of the oarsmen, nets of blue-green algae, a number of spiny fish with bristly blue or red fins, which the fishermen, thinking them true demons of the sea, threw back into the ocean or up onto dry land in order to drive misfortune away from their ships before future embarkations.

He watched for a long, long time as the underwater kingdom cast up on the shore grew still, dried up, and dissolved into memory.

In the image of the sea dream cast upon the European shore it was as though he were watching the forms of the Ottoman era cast onto the Balkans after several centuries. This image was never erased from his memory.

Holidays in Defeats

He walked late into the night along the shore of the Bosporus, now illuminated by the moon, certain that he would never again return to these shores.

In his mind, the holidays in the sultan's palaces on the Bosporus, in the marble citadel of Dolmabahçe, sprang to life.

In the nighttime, silence reigned, disturbed only intermittently by the stronger waves, which seemed to be ruled by the moon's rays.

The moon lit up the blue marble beauty, adorning its pale, deathly cladding.

In the distance seabirds foretold the future events in the life of the Balkans.

My father imagined the palace on one of the great religious or imperial holidays or during victory celebrations, most often after great defeats of Balkan nations. Here in this true cascade of crystal, gold, and silver, silk and velvet, created from the victor's spoils, was everything the empire had acquired in the Balkans, in Africa, Asia, and Europe. Here they celebrated all their victories, all our defeats. Here in these crystals culminated the splendor of a great empire, its power holding on through future victories.

When strings of defeats began to follow in ever more rapid succession, the celebrations became ever more raucous until they became ultimate defeat in this multifaceted silence, which my father, alone and exhausted, deciphered on the shores of the Bosporus, resolutely determined to trace in the Balkans the defeats of these glittering Bosporus lights and radiance.

Lost

*N*o matter how often he passed the Galata Bridge by the Golden Horn on his way to the oldest part of Constantinople, his thoughts turned once again to the great themes of the Ottoman era that would not disappear with the end of the empire.

Here at the gates of the Levant he reflected on all the European campaigns since the time of the crusaders, on all the Eastern campaigns against Europe, which shackled the Balkans in a great, five-century block of time.

He loved to come here, to walk his Balkan loneliness through this frenzied Constantinople throng, where the minor problems of his existence submerged into the great problems of this perpetually moving humanity.

Here revolutions stopped, hopes ceased, people mingled in the eternal change of moon and sun, in the continuous march of the past in a lasting contextualization of the great problems of humanity.

He wanted to mix in this mass of human oblivion that could never settle on any lasting value.

From his vantage point on the shore, Galata appeared to be the liveliest part of Constantinople. Here was the capital of capitals. Here were located the great banks, maritime companies, great trading houses—the "belly of the city," with shops of every type. Everywhere the splendor of gold seemed to spill out along the white cobblestones.

Crossing this timeless, epic bridge, entering that fluid ribbon of human motion, he continued on into the old part of Constantinople. Here was the final confluence of all races, of countless nations. It was as though he were stepping into another city, another country, another planet.

Here was no longer the hustle and bustle of Galata. The alleyways led to oases of tranquility. Here were wooden houses with high walls above which towered cypresses draped with fragrant honeysuckle, embroidering the green hedges dappled with the blue, gold, and variegated hues of Mediterranean vegetation.

This silence, this world of harmonious end points, took root in his soul for all time, and when he found himself deep in the Balkans, his thoughts would often be transplanted to these spaces. Here everything was well-formed, complete, eternal. Nearby twirled the smoke of hookahs lined up before small teahouses.

Here was where Babylon ended. Here new streams of thought would often overwhelm him; they welled up from deep within his consciousness, something deep within him, a certain disquiet at the very roots of his soul. Did all Balkan roads lead to Constantinople? Did all the dreams of past centuries, of endless generations, conclude in this empire, which was imploding before his very eyes? One paradox led to another, stronger, more encompassing, more definitive than the last. He felt like a loser in a great tournament onto whose lists he had been entered against his will.

All the laws of this empire, its faith, its great military campaigns with all their gains—all the books had to convince him that he was discovering at last his great fatherland, the fatherland of his faith. And now here he was in the very heart of that great fatherland. This fatherland had permitted him multiple fatherlands in one, but he was condemned never to discover his true one . . .

Tattered Fate

*Y*es, in Constantinople my father had his small fatherlands, his wondrous worlds, to which his soul became accustomed and poured out streams of ideas and confessions.

Afterward, lost in his thoughts, as he passed by the Great Eyüp Mosque, playfully decorated in faience and marble, animated by the flight of the pigeons circling eternally around its towering minaret, my father would turn his gaze and thoughts toward Sultan Eyüp's tomb and the Eyüp cemetery, with its countless carved turbans by the exit; he would walk along the Avenue of the Forty Stairs so he could climb up the hill from where the sight of the Golden Horn captivated the viewer.

Here was his chosen café, where he gathered his thoughts and wrote some down. This café was known to him through the novels of the famous French writer Pierre Loti, who from this vantage point preserved the great Constantinople fantasy of a bygone time, with which, in the form of Oriental exoticism, he flirted for years with his many readers, who themselves never understood the Balkan Ottoman drama.

When my father came here for the first time, he thought back on the relationship of Atatürk to such exotic novels, especially those of Pierre Loti, which looked on the Ottoman Empire only as a garden of all possible earthly delights. Atatürk was particularly troubled by the constant images in Western novels in which Muslim women were portrayed as slaves in vast harems, satisfying the frustrated Western reader's displaced dreams of a woman, forever submissive, accompanied by a splendid hookah and a box of Turkish delight.

The epoch of the exotic Aziyade as well as the mystic dervishes that intoxicated Western readers was, in Atatürk's opinion, decidedly in the past.

Here, upon this hill, beside the Golden Horn, each had his vision of Constantinople, of a time that was vanishing into the shadows of history and a time that was unfolding. Each had his own accounts to settle with his country and with this imperial city. Here each declared war or peace with Constantinople.

My father watched the intelligent steps that Atatürk made in his attempts to salvage the essential core of Turkish identity from the collapse of the Ottoman Empire. Atatürk saved what could be saved, but my father, an ordinary student from Constantinople University, with a head brimming with the statutes of sharia law and the old forms of the Ottoman administration, the Balkans' raw wounds on his mind, plus a yearning for family that pulled him toward the Balkans, what could he save?

The Turks, together with Atatürk, would turn to the core of their nation, to Anatolia, but where would my father go, where would he turn to in the Balkans, where the red-hot lava of the Ottoman Empire had flared for centuries and had not yet cooled.

Atatürk, as if with the sword of Damocles, would sever the knot of the Ottoman era and would build his country from the last bulwark of its potential identity.

Yes, Atatürk would easily free himself from the illusions of the Ottoman era, but what would become of us, his fellow citizens of the Ottoman Empire, those of us in the Balkans, where the misery of the Ottoman era would continue for a long, long time? Father contemplated this on the shores of the Bosporus before departing forever to his corner of the Balkans.

But this was not the end. The thought of what would happen to all of us in the Balkans after the fall of the Ottoman Empire completely absorbed him and remained forever part of what gave meaning to his life.

We will spend a long, long time freeing ourselves from the old deceits of the Ottoman era, from all the possible tricks used to keep us in constant conflict, to preserve the Janissary within us. He was troubled, deeply worried, about the "tattered fate" of his people and of the other peoples of the Balkans.

He saw no easy escape, but he did not want his life to be sacrificed to that Janissary curse, from which there was no hope that all the prisoners of the recent Ottoman Empire would easily be freed.

He knew how to read deep into his soul, into the souls of these people with crossed fates here in these sacred, heavenly gardens of Constantinople.

As he was returning to his condemned part of the Balkans, in his consciousness, ever more clearly, and slowly, Atatürk's final words rang out: "The future of the country seeks new people, those with a modern frame of mind."

Would his whole life pass in migration, in search of a country where he could settle down and build a family?

Where was he to find his country now that he had alienated himself from the very country everyone had told him was his? Including Atatürk himself.

My father returned to the Balkans nonetheless, where he had left his people, there in the spot where they had set down their deepest roots. He knew that he would struggle, that his life would pass along the forgotten byways of the Ottoman era, where the people were still unaware that centuries had elapsed, who did not know in what century they lived.

He knew that these people would hold fast to their new faith, more intensely than the old believers, even in its rudimentary, archaic forms, in order to survive, but at the same time they would prolong the agony of the Ottoman reign. They would sense, as he had, that the Ottoman period had reached its end. A historic mission had fallen to him, a mission that at times filled him with pride and at other times left him with an ineradicable sense of defeat.

At a time when he was not yet freed from an empire that had promised him personal salvation, peace of mind, and a restful youth, but, instead, had given him turmoil for his soul and his identity, he could not imagine that what awaited him was not only the recidivists of the old empire but the new era of the empires of Fascism and Stalinism. In that moment between the fall of the Ottoman Empire and the rise of Fascism, he could have returned to Constantinople much more easily than during Communist times.

During this period, at the end of the thirties, his mother traveled to Constantinople for the last time, for one final embrace with her surviving relatives before returning to the Balkans with the heartache that extinguished her life.

Father could not fathom that the time would come, under Stalinism, when he would not be able even to dream of Constantinople, let alone visit or return there.

In time, my father's Eastern dream turned to ashes and was swept away completely, as though Constantinople had never existed. He buried it deep, deep inside. When Stalinism collapsed in the country in which he had had the fortune to settle with his family, among the first roads to open up was the one that led to Constantinople. His body no longer possessed its youthfulness, his old dreams had been extinguished, but the first travelers to Constantinople, the traders and smugglers, came to my father carrying him greetings and some newspapers from the new era.

Yes, my father's Eastern dream was definitely buried. It remained and endured only in his many books . . .

Bartering with Fate

A good part, if not the better part, of my father's life was still ahead of him, the part in which he would interpret the enigmatic Ottoman era, the tragedy of the Janissaries, and the Ottoman script. He set aside the majority of his time for discovering the secrets held in that Perso-Arabic writing. He believed that by penetrating into the calligraphic spiral of the Ottoman script he could discover the layers of time past; he would reach the key to numerous secret records concerning the secret of the world, the universe, and the cyclical nature of civilizations. He would learn about the European Renaissance and about the old Arabic manuscripts that had preserved the wisdom of the ancients.

He saw in the old Arabic handwriting the clearest mirror of the era, of the destinies of people and nations. And now, at the end of his stay in Constantinople, someone wanted to break the mirror and then from the shards create thousands of broken mirrors. He wanted to free the mirror from the old apparitions and maledictions that emanated from the time collected within it. My father wanted to grasp this mirror, to discover in it the compressed time, the time of great misunderstandings, of defeats and victories, the time of survival. My father both did and did not comprehend Atatürk's reforms, the shift to the new Latin script. These manuscripts that had served five centuries would live on in the bygone time within them; they would remain buried in archives. But the souls of these dead manuscripts would hover in the air above the powerless souls of the living for a long, long time.

What else remained for him to hold in his memories from Constantinople? How many more times would it be necessary for him to come instinctively here to the sea, before the imposing Bosporus, to barter with his fate?

He searched out places where time was most layered, where the centuries were warehoused in manuscripts with their numerous signs and signals.

He went most often to the Topkapi museum, in particular to the libraries that held old manuscripts. It was as though he wearied of the splendor of the gold, the rubies, and the emeralds lining his pathway to the splendor of the manuscripts.

He stopped for the last time before the maze of manuscripts, from which the illusion of infinity radiated; he was transported by the illuminations, by the Sufi texts, the astrologers' texts on the wonders of the universe, the legal treatises, the essays on religion, the medical analyses, the great grammars and dictionaries, the accounts of far-off lands, the gigantic herbaria, encyclopedias, descriptions of distant parts of the empire with pictures of unknown insects, enormous bound books that recounted the legends of peoples who never existed in the past and would never exist in the future, proclamations, notes on life and on death.

It was a veritable tomb in which time lay buried, a tomb filled with life. In that section of Topkapi were also preserved the symbols of the caliphate, objects that had belonged to the prophet; but my father remained forever fascinated by the glorious manuscripts, by the memory of those books, a memory that he carried with him together with his miniatures of these books, those he had selected, back to his far corner in the Balkans, a back alleyway of expired Ottoman times.

After the splendor of Topkapi, the thought of the Balkan gloom lingered with him. He often circled the Blue Mosque, and, above his head, he watched the waves of blue pigeons with their open wings; in the sea of his memory, they would remind him always of this part of Constantinople's changing past.

Everything he could carry away from this time he would place in the books he prepared for exile to his native Balkans, which, although until yesterday united in one of the great distorted mirrors of the Topkapi Palace, now lay shattered into shards of peoples, nations, and destinies.

What other choice did he really have than to set off from this city of his youth, in which he would leave behind close relatives whom he would never see again, perhaps some unfinished youthful romance?

He carried away only the books, his most important possessions, as if carrying in them the entire Ottoman era, which would later in the Balkans be left to him to unfold, to augment, to which he would summon the people to bear witness in a sort of mutual catharsis, that all had not been lost in that now-vanished time . . .

The Dream of the Books

*I*t is not possible, it will never be possible, for a single war to solve the problems of an era. No matter how big it is, no matter how just for some and unjust for others, war will impose new borders. What if these borders sever the souls of people, families, gardens, dreams, time, the people's time? What is left for these people who are condemned to the hell within the borders of Babylon other than to accustom themselves calmly to their destiny? To build a new home in Babel . . .

When my father returned from Constantinople, he remained forever entangled in the Balkan borderlines. With great luck he stayed alive and just managed to get his family across several borders, but deep within him the last flickering of his Constantinople nights was extinguished.

Later, after Stalinism ended, somewhere around the 1960s, when the borders were at last opened and it was possible once again to travel to Constantinople, we children thought that my father would finally go there; he would get to go to Constantinople before his death and so complete the great dream he had dreamed in fragments through those terrible years in the Balkans spent rescuing his family.

We children felt a rush of happiness that our father's travel to Constantinople could be renewed. To us, oppressed by the evenly distributed poverty of the Socialist years, Constantinople now appeared as a possible escape. After thirty years of silence the first news arrived from relatives there. Among the first to head off to Constantinople were the accomplished traders and—need I even say it—the Socialist smugglers. The first letters started to arrive, the first calls, but my father never revealed their secret to us.

When regular bus service was established between our city and Constantinople, we became ever more impatient to pick the day to send our father on his second voyage there, to the city of his youth, while his body still supported him.

My father avoided discussions about his possible trip to Constantinople. We had known before that he did not like to talk about the years of his youth in Constantinople. He acted as if he had never even been there. But we understood when, in the middle of his Balkan nights, in the eye of the radio that he had brought from Constantinople and dragged along on all our Balkan resettlements as if it were an equal member of the family, he searched for a certain Constantinople radio station to find that enchanting instrumental and vocal music, that Eastern spirituality, which, it seemed, drew him to distant places. We knew that something powerful had happened to him in his youth in Constantinople, something that marked him for his whole life. It was as if he had sworn never to return to that city again.

One day, my oldest brother, having waited a long time for my father to reveal to us the secret of his life in Constantinople, asked him impatiently, "So, Dad, the country has opened up. Everyone is traveling to Constantinople. How come you aren't going to see your people now while you still can, now that we are already on our own two feet?"

Our father was and was not surprised by this question. He found himself in the center of the "Constantinople conspiracy" that the family had prepared for him.

Sometimes he confided in my mother about his life there, but only in the few words whose content was well known to all the family. But we children wanted to go further than our mother in resolving our father's Constantinople enigma.

My father met my oldest brother's gaze. There was a flash in my father's blue eyes, eyes that reassured us whenever life brought us face to face with his wisdom. Now he restrained himself an instant as if seeking those few but true words that could tell the whole truth; then he said,

"My son, there are places in the world where one travels only once, lest the second trip betray the first."

And that was it. That was as much as we would learn of the enigma of Father's time in Constantinople. Father's sparse explanation remained for us to interpret throughout our lifetimes.

All of us children, our close relatives, our neighbors, we all traveled to Constantinople, first by train or by bus and later in our small Fiats. But it was a different Constantinople. My father's Constantinople remained perhaps only in his books. In Father's books . . .

The Eastern Sword
of Damocles

*F*or a long time my father kept his meeting with Atatürk out of his biography, especially during the Stalinist era. He hid it even from us children. His wisdom in life was based on his power to conceal the truth when all those close to him thought it should be told. My father almost never became a slave to words misspoken.

While studying in Constantinople, my father had the good fortune to be invited through his mother's relatives to stay with an illustrious family, one involved in the fate of the new Turkey. This was his relative Fethi Okyar Bey, also known as the president in Atatürk's government. During my father's studies he lived with Fethi Bey's family. He studied sharia law in old Turkish, that is, the Ottoman language.

His meeting with Atatürk, made possible by his illustrious relative, marked his life forever, touching something deeply profound in him. My father had tremendous respect for the public figure of Atatürk. He was thrilled by his great historic courage to cut through the tangled knot of the Ottoman era using his Eastern sword of Damocles. My father, on the other hand, was a captive of his old Eastern dream. His great love affair with the Ottoman script began during the time of his studies in Constantinople. He fell captive to the magical calligraphy, which, like a spiral staircase, led him up the endless steps to God. These challenging lines of the old Ottoman script, of the Eastern Gordian knot, formed the labyrinth in which time had stopped and before whose exit Atatürk stood with sword in hand. Yes, it was the time when the sun was setting on the dream of the old Ottoman Turkish script. What was sunset for Atatürk was sunrise for my father. For some it was a lost time, for others a time yet to be revealed. But all were condemned, lost in the labyrinth of time, powerless before the relativity of time's passage.

"History is always tragic," said my father, remembering Atatürk's words.

My father's return to the heart of the Balkans after the fall of the Ottoman Empire meant an end to one dream and the beginning of another. His life unfolded between these two dreams.

As much as he agreed with some of Atatürk's ideas, he disagreed with others. Father agreed in principle with Atatürk's view that "it was necessary to carry out more than one revolution" in order to escape from the Ottoman era. But while my father did think it necessary to carry out more than one revolution, he viewed this fact in relation to past times. It was as if they dreamed the same Eastern dream, but in different temporal directions.

Atatürk, according to my father, claimed that Islam was a religion alien to the Turkish nation, a foreign entity grafted onto the organism, the revenge of the victorious clergy over the military victors! My father thought that Atatürk was perhaps correct in his efforts to secularize the new Turkish society. But he held a somewhat different point of view: if victors had imposed Islam on the Turks, then the Turks, in turn, had imposed it on the peoples they defeated.

Did my father now have the right to seek a double revolution? Yes: here in the Balkans there remained immense spiritual, moral, and political arenas for a historic settling of accounts. Here were new crossroads leading to labyrinths of possible new defeats. One victory alone is not a definitive conquest, nor is one defeat a definitive rout. He worried that, one day, playing with this dream of religion in the Balkans would become the singular refuge of the people, leading to a hundred years of religious conflict. My father was deeply worried about the fate of the Balkans. He did not have a mighty pen of truth as Atatürk had a sword of victory.

The Fedora

The history of his people stopped at the shores of this wondrous lake with the most translucent waters in the world, with kingdoms of algae in which the silver trout reigned supreme. It was said that this lake was a million years old. The lake was sacred. Its waves were awaited on the shore like whispers of eternity. Everything of significance that occurred in the lives of these people occurred on the shores of the lake. People set off from the shore of the lake, people returned to the shore of the lake. The lives of these people were passed amid the departures and returns of their close family, their closest kin.

Every departure was mourned, every return celebrated. Though the reverse could happen, too; everything depended on the fate of the people. When someone who had worked in America returned, a large crowd usually gathered on the shore of the lake; there were relatives, both near and distant, passersby, poor folk, a beggar or two. When these workers returned from Constantinople or Bucharest, from Cairo or Budapest, the number of people gathered was no less. Many of those at these gatherings waited for news of a family member; close relatives expected presents; the children hoped for candies and sweets; the beggars pleaded for alms. Everyone expected something. But these moments of return were what they were, sad or joyful, moments for remembrance or forgetting, for praise or condemnation.

When my father returned to his native town from Constantinople, there were many people present. Not only were our nearest and dearest kin there, but so were also several of our more distant relatives, those who had quarreled with my father over the division of some land. Many people came, some out of happiness, others out of envy. My father had spent a long time, a very long time, in Constantinople. Four years, to be precise, a whole lifetime for his mother, for his old father, for all his brothers and sisters. His mother had sent him to Constantinople, to her relatives, because she wanted to distance him from the family and its tribal quarrels. She wanted him to see another world, the Bosporus, to see Constantinople, to see the city of her youth and her close family, which was dispersed throughout the Balkans.

And now everyone was here by the lake to welcome my father home. Everyone had his own opinion about the return, each according to his own perspective. The older ones expected to see my father in a fez. The younger ones knew that Atatürk had banned the fez, and they believed that my father would come wearing the Albanian white cap on his head or nothing at all. Some of the oldest folks believed that they would see him wearing the distinctive signs of someone who had made the hajj, since they thought that one could quickly and easily get to Mecca from Constantinople. They expected to see him with presents; the children expected sweets of varying kinds. Only the children felt happy . . .

Everybody was surprised when my father stepped out of an ordinary carriage in which there was barely enough room for his two large suitcases. They expected also a cart with his possessions and his presents, but there was none to be seen. My father betrayed the expectations of many people.

First of all, he did not emerge and step out onto the ground in a fez or a turban, in a white cap, or with his head bare. Instead, he wore a fedora, sporting clothing cut to the latest European fashion.

There were sentiments of barely concealed surprise and disapproval. Many of the people were seeing a fedora for the first time, and those who had seen one had done so only once before, when an Italian magician was visiting the town. Everyone was astonished; various thoughts went through their minds. My father, too, was surprised, but he wore the fedora until the end of his life.

Surely he must have gold, silver, and other precious objects in his suitcases, the more distant relatives noted quietly.

He must have a lot of money! Four years just hanging out in Stamboul, you can put together real money! others chimed in.

His closest family ran up. His mother, with tears of joy in her eyes, approached him first. They warmly embraced. Here was someone who rejoiced at his homecoming. Then he hugged his sisters. His brothers carried the large suitcases, which they unlocked and opened with ease, before my father got there. The suitcases were opened, and out came many books, manuscripts. My father's books.

"Ohhhh, it's books!" the oldest cried.

"Holy books!" added others when they saw the old Ottoman script of the manuscripts, which they recognized from the Koran.

"He wasted his time in Stamboul," tossed in a third.

⁐

So the life of my father's books in the Balkans began with misunderstanding, and from none other than his own family. The old rivals in the family, from that same distant branch, heard these rebukes with hidden pleasure, without involving themselves in the conversation. But so be it, the books would definitely separate my father from them and later from his birthplace. The books became animate objects in my father's life; they marked out a pathway for his life. My father accepted the destiny of the books. And there was no longer anyone who could sway him from this path. During dreadful events that occurred in the Balkans, he took up the books as living companions, advisors; they brought him comfort to the end of his life.

So began the fate of Father's books in the Balkans. In the beginning, the books kept Father distant from people, but later they brought him closer. The people who greeted him on the shore of the lake began by asking among themselves and with their close and distant relatives what my father might be hiding in these books. What were his plans? You couldn't raise a family with books. He could not even be a Balkan Don Quixote. It was difficult to find one's Sancho Panza, and, what's more, there weren't any windmills.

Friends and relatives both near and far came to ask my father whether there was any news, what was happening with their close family and their more distant kin. They came and cast a secret glance at the books. Even close family came after hearing the tales of others that my father had fogged his brain with books in Constantinople, and now he had returned with them to do the same to others. There were those who asked whether he had earned money and then spent it in Constantinople's houses of ill repute. My father calmly answered all their questions; for everyone he had a calm and comforting word. His mother first responded in anger to the questions of these ill-mannered guests, but when she saw with what intelligence and composure her son answered them, she felt joy and warmth in her soul. She was happy most of all that her son had returned alive and healthy, with his intellect and with his books.

The first days after Father's return passed. Others who had gone abroad to work returned to the shores of the lake. Father's return with his books seemed to fall into oblivion. My father saw to it that the books were well hidden in one room in the attic, where he secretly went and remained a long, long time with his books.

Time Discovered

$\mathcal{B}$efore my eyes were all his old books, his manuscripts, maps, notes, notebooks, old geographic maps, and proclamations, those that had been read and those left unfinished. There were those that had been studied and those that remained unexamined. All had a significance that extended through time.

All of Father's books could be read as one book, the book of his life. I was left to page once again through a life, the history of one journey transfused into me and into the new era of the family.

In these books and notes my father had carried his Ottoman time, later to unpack it in that part of the Balkans where he would set down roots for his whole life. He knew that this era had not completely flowed out of the Balkans.

These books would follow my father through the collapse of several kingdoms and empires. The books outlived eras; they outlived my father as well. I remained powerless to interpret them; I followed a different route through other languages and cultures. Yet, I know very well that much of my father remains in them—his spirit, his unspoken admonitions and advice. The books contain streams of time not yet past. With these books one could collect the currents of past times. These books enchant because they stand outside of time. They revived within me my father's illusions and his powerlessness to build from them the truth. I do not know where these books will end. When our life ends, what of us remains in the books that we have read? . . .

Documents I

*I*n Mother's soul, the hands of some great clock advanced—most often by the sound of Father's footsteps, that distinctive tread on the cobblestones distinguished easily from others'. The sound of those footsteps noticeably calmed her and brought peace to the household.

This continued for years. My mother remembered my father's frequent departures before and during wartime, when he prepared a strategy for the family's next resettlement. Now times were different, but, for my mother, the times stayed always the same.

If Father's time of arrival changed, Mother suspected immediately that something had happened to him. Once something did happen. Without notifying us ahead of time, my father was late getting home, very, very late. My mother was overcome with an unrest that was soon transferred to us children as well. Time passed quickly; it was getting dark, and there was no sign of my father at all. Night fell; no one could sleep a wink. At daybreak, my oldest brother set off for the Institute of National History, where my father worked. All of us at home calmed down when we learned that my father had unexpectedly left for the south in search of some old Ottoman documents, documents he had been seeking his entire life, ever since the fall of the Ottoman Empire, when, studying from books with old Ottoman Turkish, or Perso-Arabic, script, he completed a law program in Constantinople.

After years of persistent searching he had come at last to his great discovery: Ottoman documents with which a part of the lost history of the Balkans could be reconstructed, the history of forgotten families, the great web of our history. He felt deeply within him that he had reached a quiet victory at last.

When he left Constantinople in the twenties of the last century, he held in his hands his diploma for his completed degree in sharia law. He examined the calligraphy in the old script, the markings on his diploma that were to lead him, by some internal diktat, back to his people in the Balkans, to his imagined battle with lost time. All this was in spite of the fact that Atatürk had already confirmed the fall of the Ottoman Empire, had established the Latin alphabet as the new Turkish script, and had proposed a series of other reforms that marked the conclusive end of the Ottoman era. Thus my father found himself imprisoned in a maze of two scripts, Latin and Arabic. He knew very well the way out of the Arabic arabesque, but he was not prepared to accept Atatürk's challenge and to accept a position (likely a high one) in the new government hierarchy in the new Turkey. . . . As a young man in Constantinople he had found himself at the true intersection of eras, faiths, nations, the ruins of a five-century empire. He was also at the entrance to his own personal labyrinth. He well knew that in this crucible of past time the history of his family's identity was melted together with that of his predecessors, his nation, the peoples in the Balkans who had lived together for centuries. After the defeat of the Ottoman era, my father was aware that his own victory over the past was possible.

That refrain that passed from generation to generation in the Balkans—"who has stolen our time?"—reached his generation as well; but time was stolen in the new eras in the Balkans as well: the Balkan wars, the First and then the Second World Wars, the Stalinist era. He knew that his battle with the Ottoman era was first of all personal and only then a shared one. He had to win, to discover the path toward the lost Ottoman time . . .

He felt as though he had found his Atlantis of documents. He fully believed that these dead manuscripts would one day rise up and release all the lost memory of his people and of all the other peoples in the Balkans. He was lucky that now the dream of his youth had returned to be realized in his mature years. And so he determined to devote the remaining part of his life to these newly discovered manuscripts.

Now, after all the past storms, after having survived the fall of the Ottoman kingdom, the fall of Fascism, the fall of Stalinism, he had found an oasis of peace, acceptance, and tolerance where his old dream would unfold until the end of his life.

Documents II

$\mathcal{M}$y mother intuitively sensed my father's next steps, when fate offered no choice. They had spent so much of their lives together, avoiding the same traps, that they created some sort of agreement, a shared sense of life's weight, as if one continued into the other, and in that tenacity we children grew up, stood on our own, and matured.

My mother surely knew by now that my father had at last reached his life's great discovery in his search for the manuscripts. Only such a discovery could have put him into a state such as she had never before seen in his life.

During his frequent archival searches among possible sources of Ottoman manuscripts in Macedonia, my father had noticed in a Bitola mosque two nailed-shut boxes stuffed with notebooks, manuscripts, and papers. From one of the partially opened boxes he was able to examine several sheets of paper. He opened the box, barely able to cope with the centuries of dust stirred up from the notebooks. Thinking they were holy books, no one had wanted to commit a sin by carrying the manuscripts out of the mosque; as a result, they had survived conflagration and war.

As he began to turn the pages of these account books, my father was immediately transported into another temporal stream. There was no lost time, there was no lost time, he said aloud to himself.

At first, the imam was upset as he watched my father handle these "holy books," but he then calmed down because he believed that everything in these manuscripts had been foretold, including my father's arrival. My father began to read aloud to the imam from the old notes in a clear and pure diction, fluently and with feeling.

The imam now understood that these had nothing to do with sacred texts. My father read and recited the Koran to him as only my father knew how. My father's reading pleasantly surprised the imam. My father quickly gained the imam's confidence . . .

Documents III

*M*y father immediately contacted the archives about his great discovery. He asked them to inform his family that he would remain another day on the road. The courier from the archives who should have called had a drink somewhere en route and did not get to our house until the next day, after my older brother had already gone to find out what had happened to our father.

My father was immediately given the go-ahead by the highest authority to review the documents and have them transferred to the National Archives. It was not easy for him to convince the imam to transfer the documents to another place after they had remained so many centuries in that holy place. My father clearly explained to him that these documents were administrative court documents that somehow or other had ended up in the mosque. The imam, who also knew Arabic script from the Koran, now assured that these were not holy books, allowed my father, after three hundred promises not to dispose of the books, to take them and inform the imam of their future fate. My father agreed, and they parted as friends.

My mother, carried away by the day's events, forgot her many pressing worries and, perhaps for the first time, did not notice when my father arrived home with his traveling bag. He was tired from not having slept the night before, but in his face there was a new expression, one that none of us in the house had ever seen. Maybe he had worn such an expression once or twice a year, when we children brought our report cards home with excellent grades at the end of the school year or when my mother brought him a book he had long been seeking. But, to all of us, it was clear as day that something significant had happened to him that would mark the remainder of his life. It was clear that he had found an exit from the labyrinth of manuscripts that led out into life.

When he had regained his strength and the family had returned to its daily rituals, my father got to work on the pile of archival documents from the mosque. Time truly resided in them.

The Meaning
of the Silence

When my brothers were approaching adulthood and our only sister was ready to be engaged to be married, my father was once again gripped by the Eastern dream, like the one he had when he left Constantinople in the twenties; he could not imagine that historical events would diverge so much from the course he had predicted for them.

He had been certain that one day he would return to Constantinople, would resume his former Eastern time, would return to the smell of the dried honeysuckle blossoms and of the faded flowers in the white jasmine gardens.

He could not believe that time would be suspended forever between him and Constantinople, that he would never again return to that city.

In fact, the country in which he settled was the first to be freed from Stalinism and opened to the world, including, of course, Constantinople. My father could go there whenever he wanted. But before he went, merchants and black marketeers traveled there, and they destroyed the picture of Constantinople that he had imagined and that was secured forever in his soul.

His children matured and were ready for advanced studies. As soon as one would graduate and begin to work, the next child would be ready to go. And so on in order . . .

The whole family seemed to be in constant flux almost to the end of my father's life. Perhaps, deep within him, he lived with the illusion that at least one of his sons would leave, to continue studies in Cairo or Constantinople, to reconnect with my father's youth. It was difficult to carry out such a plan in the Balkans, in the country that had fenced itself in. Nevertheless, my father fed our illusions of setting off after his lost dream, especially when it became our time for study or marriage. He wanted to connect at least one of us, a vain hope, with his Eastern dream, while others, more disturbed Stalinists than Stalin himself, concerned themselves with the dream of Father's native land, the last in the Balkans to destroy the giant monument to Stalin. His native land was condemned to the greatest isolation in the Balkans, in the world. It was covered entirely in bunkers. Yes, my father was sure that even there the winds of democracy would blow at some time, but he did not live to see it.

My father could not force his way on us, but something unspoken remained in his life, something that he keenly wanted to tell us. His silence remained the greatest narrative of our lives.

The Documents
(Epilogue)

*M*y father searched once again for the lost Ottoman time in the Balkans, for his own delight, as he often said, but his friends, schooled Orientalists, specialists in Turkology, would say to him that it was a historical mission. The day would come, they told him, when the countries that emerged after the fall of the Ottoman Empire would fatefully seek out documents concerning their identity, an identity preserved for centuries.

After my father rescued the documents from the mosque and set them in order, he dedicated the remainder of his life to them. For twenty years my father tended to that bundle of yellowed paper that could easily have ended as dust and ashes. He discovered messages written on the old official documents, and he wrote them anew onto small note cards. Thousands of them! In this way this material was tamed, prepared for its exit from the old era to the new.

My father built his Ottoman Babylon page by page. Balkan Babel, as his true friend, Mr. K., called it. For the remainder of his life, my father dedicated himself completely to his battle with the old manuscripts, which threatened to vanish completely if one did not devote to them sufficient patience. And patience was what my father had most of all in his life.

The people around my father grasped the historical significance of this rescued pile of yellowed paper. My father had no other ambitions; he just continued his quiet friendship with the old documents; he dispersed the treasures of these old documents; for days and nights he translated from the documents for those who studied the Turkish period in the history of the Balkan nations. Those grateful to him thanked him in the footnotes of their scholarly works and dissertations, but later they omitted his name. It was only when he was completely worn out by diabetes during his battle with the papers that he went on disability pension and separated definitively from his old documents. Others took them and continued to translate and publish them. They eventually came to the translations my father had made on the note cards. On them nearly every document had been interpreted. While working for a newspaper, I happened to come across the finished manuscript of the translation of the court records in a publishing house.

I look and see my father's familiar records, his translations. His name is not listed with the others on the book. I race home. My father is recovering with difficulty because of his last stroke. Once again he is bent over some books. I see my mother, worried. She tells me not to disturb him with new books. But I cannot act in any other way, and I tell him about my discovery in the publishing house.

My father stands with difficulty, he holds on to his cane, he goes over to the typewriter, he inserts a sheet of paper, and he types the first words: "A great breach of copyright . . ."

He cannot go on. He loses his last strength, and I curse myself for having brought him the news. My mother worriedly grabs him and looks at me with reproach. I am comforted by the thought that if I had not told my father about the event, we would have been tormented by the silence even more. So what had to happen happened! But deep inside I was afraid that I would lose my father over this. Just what he needed—one more worry, and that would be the end of him.

I leave my father in peace. I take the sheet of paper with my father's incomplete request. The next day I stop in at the archives. I tell them that an oversight had occurred, that it was not fair. One of the directors tells me that my father had translated the documents while he was working in the archives during the course of his working hours—but for my father, the poor man, his whole life was his work time, as far as I knew. I tell the director that copyright, an author's rights, remains copyright regardless of anything else. He tells me that my father should come to the archives so they could discuss it. I tell him that if they did not yet understand, they were never going to understand.

The next day I go to see my father. He greets me calmly. I see him composed; he has slept well, and I am filled with pleasure. My mother is also calm. I show him the complaint about the oversight of his copyright privileges. He takes the paper, he reads it carefully, and then he tears it up, throws it into the trash, and says to me with composure, "Son, I have decided not to submit a complaint."

I look at him in amazement. He continues: "The court documents allowed me to accomplish everything I wanted to in my life. Thanks to them, all you children grew up, you were all educated . . ."

In the room silence prevailed. For the first time in my life I saw him with tears in his eyes, or at least that is how it appeared to me.

Perhaps
the Real Ending

A Borrowed Book

My father treated his books as if they were sacred objects. He lent books from his library only to those readers he believed worthy of reading them, and then he did not worry at all whether the books were returned to him. The books were always returned to him.

For nearly his whole life, my father read with a pencil in his hand, gently underlining the rows or marking along the margins. The lines were nearly imperceptible, and they faded with time. But when he stopped reading with a pencil, we sensed that something deep inside him was dying out. When for several days he held in his hands a half-closed book, a large dictionary, a quiet sadness descended on the house.

When he no longer had the strength to hold the book in his hands, he called my mother and told her something significant. Setting aside the last book he would read in his lifetime, gathering up his remaining strength, Father collected his last mental powers: he reviewed the order of the books in the library he had not visited for a long time. Several of the books in it were not his; they stuck out on the shelves of his memory. With the final words of his life, he asked my mother to go to his library, find the books he had borrowed, and return them to their owners that very day.

My mother, who her whole life had tolerated Father's boundless enthusiasm for his books, obediently, as always during this half century of their life together, left my father on his deathbed to carry out this wish as well, not believing it to be his last.

When my father saw my mother open the door after returning the books, he had just enough strength to close his eyes for the last time.